I0684652

COLD CASE: FBI

The Salem Witch

Timminy Press | Springfield, MA USA

Other books by William Dusty:
The *Stellar Conflict* series:
> Friends and Enemies
> The Quiet World
> Predator in Our Midst
> The Girl with the Strange Green Eyes
> Sebastian's Prize

ISBN-13: 978-0-692-84872-2
Published by Timminy Press
Springfield, Massachusetts USA | 2017
www.timminypress.com

Shutterstock images by Netfalls Remy Musser, Andrey Popov, Martin Novak. Additional images by William Dusty.

Table of Contents

- - -

Dedicated to the victims of domestic violence.

****

"Make sure you're in bed by eleven thirty, Becky," Suzanne Kerch said to her teenaged daughter. "I have to talk to John alone."

The thirty-something mother busied herself washing dishes in the kitchen while her teenaged daughter carried a basket of clothes down from the second floor on her way to the laundry room in the basement.

"Come on, Mom," Becky said back to her. "You guys are *always* fighting. Why can't we just leave him for good and get our own place?"

Suzanne laughed at that. "Yeah. Right. On my income? Don't you want a car after you get your driver's license?"

Becky stopped, then detoured over to the kitchen's entrance. She looked at her mother. "I want to get out of this house a lot more, Mom. John's an asshole. He treats you like shit."

Suzanne scowled at her daughter. "Watch your language, young lady. Remember who you're talking to."

Becky rolled her eyes. The situation at home, for her, was getting unbearable.

"If he hits you again," she said, "I'm calling the cops."

Suzanne glared at her. "Don't you start up again, Rebecca. I'll handle everything. You just need to stay out of it. I don't need him getting pissed off at the both of us."

"What? And hitting *me*, too?" Becky asked.

Suzanne sighed, frustrated by her daughter's rebelliousness. She turned to the sink and slapped her sponge into the water. "I'm talking to him tonight," she said. "We'll see what happens. Just do the laundry and try to get up to bed before he gets home tonight."

Becky started off again. She huffed under her breath,

"Yeah," as she went back to the staircase.

Suzanne picked up her sponge and went back to washing dishes. She had a lot on her mind that night, and something very big to settle with her boyfriend, John, as well. It was getting late, and she knew he'd be home in another hour or so.

Things were going to change, she decided. They had to.

And this time, she finally had the upper hand.

1

Gone But Not Forgotten

It was a warm summer weekend in July of 2004 when Suzanne Kerch and her only child, Rebecca, disappeared from their Hadley, Massachusetts home, where they had lived for several years with Suzanne's boyfriend, John Henneger, who owned the place. No one had seen or heard from either of the two women ever since. The Massachusetts State Police had long ago concluded that the two women were murdered, but with no bodies having turned up, their investigation seemingly reached an endpoint. Their only person of interest, Henneger, claimed that the two women had left him that weekend—this despite the fact that Suzanne's car and much of her belongings remained behind at the house. Suzanne, furthermore, had called a friend that Saturday night at about 9:00 PM, and in that conversation there had been no mention of her going anywhere.

The Monday morning following the Kerchs' disappearance, Suzanne's workplace called her to find out why she hadn't come to work. No one answered the phone. After another couple of days of absence then, her boss called the police that Wednesday. Local police, in turn, called Henneger's home that same morning. Again, though, no one answered. A police cruiser then stopped by, but the officer, Patrolman James Banning, saw nothing unusual. No one answered a knock on the door. He did take note of an old green minivan parked off to the side of the driveway, but, peering through the windows, saw nothing inside that looked out of place. Later that same day then, police called again. This time Henneger was home, and they asked him about the whereabouts of the two women. Henneger told them that he had been out drinking with some friends that Saturday night, and by the time he got home they were already gone from the house. He didn't know where they'd gone to, but he admitted he and Suzanne had fought a lot, so it was possible she'd finally got fed up with him and left. He advised they check with Suzanne's sister. The police did not search the property at that time.

Suzanne's sister, Sandy Whiting, meanwhile, after being contacted by the police, drove up from her home in Middlefield, Connecticut, the following morning to search the area for herself. This was a Thursday—five days after the women had gone missing the previous weekend. Whiting had asked the local police to search Henneger's property at that time, but to no avail. It was only after a full week had gone by—on that following Saturday—that police conducted a formal search of the property. By then, though, much to Whiting's frustration, Henneger would have had plenty of time to remove any evidence from the site.

In statements made to the media shortly after the women's disappearance, Henneger again asserted that Suzanne and Becky had left his house sometime prior to his getting home. He didn't contact the police, he said, because the two women would often go off for days at a time without contacting him—a story Sandy Whiting found hard to believe, but couldn't prove false.

A couple of days after the initial investigation began, the Massachusetts State Police got involved. The same as their local counterparts, however, they failed to uncover any clues leading to the possible whereabouts or fate of the missing women. Some months later, then, the active investigation—which included dragging parts of the

Connecticut River and searching a nearby landfill—slipped into cold case purgatory.

John Henneger himself, meanwhile, was later arrested and convicted on drug dealing charges, resulting in a three-year stay in prison before he got out on parole. He left Hadley soon after his release, moving a short distance away, to the small city of Northampton.

****

Marvin Ledds sat back in his chair at the Kozy Kitchen, a small diner on Northampton Street in Holyoke, Massachusetts. After an overnight stay at a local motel, he'd stopped in for a quick breakfast and cup of coffee before hitting the road again for the drive down Interstate 91, on his way to Bradley International Airport.

Ledds was a paunchy, middle-aged African-American man with a balding head of graying hair. He donned a pair of thin, wire-rimmed glasses as he perused the local newspaper while eating at his table. He'd just read up on the ten-year anniversary of the disappearance and suspected murder of a mother and daughter from the nearby town of Hadley.

Ten years, he pondered, *and no leads in the case.*

A young waitress came up to Ledds' table carrying a carafe of coffee.

"More coffee, sir?" she asked him politely.

"No," he answered. "I'm all set. I'll take my check, please."

"Alrighty," the waitress replied, and she left to retrieve his bill.

Ledds folded up the newspaper and tucked it under his arm as he got up from his chair. The waitress returned with his check, and he finished off his coffee before taking it from her. He eyed it, quickly tabulated the tip, and then set the check on the table as he pulled out his wallet to pay.

"You folks ever hear anything about the disappearance of that mom and her daughter from the town across the way here?" he asked the waitress.

The town of Hadley lay just across the Connecticut River and upstream from Holyoke. Ledds had been reading the *Springfield Ledger*, a local weekly out of the nearby city of Springfield, which in this edition included the story on the disappearance of Suzanne and Rebecca Kerch.

"Oh, is that from that article there?" asked the waitress, pointing at the newspaper.

"Yeah, the Hadley girls." Ledds nodded.

"I never heard anything about it. But that was a long time ago. That's so sad what happened to them. Everyone knows her boyfriend did it. But the police can't find anything on him."

Ledds gathered up his money along with the check, and handed it to the waitress. "Thanks," he said. "Have a good day."

"You, too. Thanks much."

Ledds left the diner and strode over to his rental car—a blue Toyota Corolla which he had parked on the street. He got in and started it up. He drummed his fingers on the steering wheel, deep in thought. Too much time had passed, he figured, between the girls' disappearance and the cops showing up to search the boyfriend's place.

What were they waiting for?

Ledds reached for his belt-fastened phone clip and took up his smartphone. He thumbed around the menu to get to his contacts, then tapped on the initials "JW" listed there. He brought the phone up to his ear as it began to ring.

After a moment, the voice of a woman answered. "Hello there, Mister Ledds," she said.

"Miss Weirdlee," he replied. "And how are you on this fine day?"

"Just wonderful," she said. "What can I do for the boss man today?"

Ledds smiled. A career special agent with the FBI's Criminal, Cyber, Response, and Services Branch, Ledds had been promoted to head up that same branch some years ago. Joanna Weirdlee was one of his top intelligence analysts whom he had recruited straight out of Brandeis University just a year ago. She was a slim woman of about medium height, with long, straight, dark red hair. In normal conversation, she spoke in a calm, almost monotone voice, with a decidedly Bostonian accent. She also had a reputation for being quite the mystery woman. No one really knew anything about her history—except for Ledds himself, that is. But he wasn't talking.

"I want you to come up to New England this week, my dear," he said to her. "I have some work for you here."

"You're letting me out of my cage?" Weirdlee replied, surprised.

Weirdlee had been working out of the J. Edgar Hoover Building for the past year, since coming out of college. Ledds had told her that he was grooming her for field duty, although for the longest time that opportunity never seemed to materialize.

Until now.

"I think it's time to set you free, Joanna."

"*Nice*," Weirdlee replied. "Are you still in New Hampshire?"

"No, I drove down to Holyoke, Mass, this morning to visit an old friend of mine working for the police here. Listen, I want you to come up and do some preliminary work. It's about a couple of missing persons, going on ten years now in a town across the river from where I am. I can email you the details after I catch my flight out of Bradley."

"*Summertime...in New England,*" Weirdlee sang. "I'll start packing."

"Good.—Oh, and I also want you to contact that hot shot from our New York City office. What's his name? Nichols? I want him on this one. Tell him I'll be calling him this week."

"You don't want someone from the Boston office?"

"Nah. I heard good things about this guy. I think we'll need him on this one."

"Okay, boss. You got it."

"Talk to you soon," said Ledds.

He tapped off his phone and replaced it on his belt clip. Bradley International Airport was a half an hour away over the Massachusetts-Connecticut border. With any luck, he'd be back in Washington, DC before noon.

2

Returning to the Past

BROOKLYN, NEW YORK

"Can I meet you downtown for lunch?"

Special Agent Danny Fielding stood in front of the bathroom mirror straightening out his tie. His wife, Kara, stood leaning in the doorway, dressed in her bathrobe and smiling at her man.

"Sure, I think so," he said to her.

Both husband and wife shared a pronounced Southern accent, lending to their common upbringing in Arkansas where the two grew up and went to high school together.

Kara eased up next to her husband and wrapped an arm over his shoulder. She looked at his reflection in the mirror, still smiling. "That sure is a handsome man in there," she said.

Fielding smiled back at his wife's image in the mirror. "I think he's with that sexy woman standing next to him, though."

"That bitch," Kara replied with a fake scowl.

Fielding turned and kissed her on the lips. Then he stepped around her to leave the bathroom, bringing her in tow.

"I got a call earlier, babes," he said to her, making his way over to their dining room table to retrieve his jacket. "I may have to head up to Massachusetts for a couple days. Maybe a bit longer, depending."

The couple lived in a small, two-bedroom townhouse apartment in Brooklyn, with their 2-year-old son, Emmett, taking up the second bedroom. The kitchen area adjoined the dining room, both separated by a waist-high divider. A small living room was set off to the right of the dining room, where the apartment's front door was located. The couple's home computer and a study desk were set in the back corner of the living room, just behind a small couch that faced their home entertainment center.

"Something important? A case?"

"Oh, it's a ten-year-old missing persons case," said Fielding, pulling on his jacket. "A mother and her daughter gone missing. Assistant Director Ledds himself put us on it. We're going up there to snoop around, see if there's anything we can do."

Kara approached Fielding and rested her hands on his chest, patting the lapels of his jacket. "You getting along okay with your new partner?" she asked him.

"We're all right, I guess," he replied with a mild sigh that hinted otherwise. "He's not the warmest sort of guy."

"Oh? A hard ass, is he?"

"Nah, I wouldn't say that," Fielding said as he gathered up his black leather briefcase and checked his smartphone for the time. "He just doesn't show a whole lot of emotion. The guy never really smiles, and he keeps to himself at the office."

Kara folded her arms in front of her chest. "Maybe he's been around the block a few times and just doesn't like to small talk."

"He's got no personality, is what it is," Fielding shot back. He stood in front of his wife and gave her another peck on the lips. "Anyway, we'll be heading out either Friday or Saturday, depending on what that Weirdlee girl finds out for us up there."

"Weirdlee..." Kara pondered. "What a strange name for a person."

Fielding smiled at her. "Weird, right?"

He walked to the door then to leave. Kara followed close behind him. He opened the door and gave her a cursory hug before stepping out. "I'll see you for lunch, hon. You pick the place and text me."

"Sure thing, sweets. See you this afternoon."

****

MIDDLEFIELD, CONNECTICUT

Sandy Whiting lived in a pleasant neighborhood in Middlefield, Connecticut, along with her husband, Richard, and their daughter, Paula. It was early evening, still, and presently she sat at her kitchen table inside of her home, joined there by a couple of visiting friends. The upcoming Saturday was Paula's sixteenth birthday, and Sandy was planning an afternoon yard party for her at their house. Sandy's friends had come by to help her get things organized.

"Whatever we do, we gotta watch for any boys coming over, trying to bring in beer or whatever," said Tracy Fallon, probably Sandy's least favorite friend.

Sandy shook her head dismissively. "There aren't going to be any boys. Teenage boys wouldn't be caught dead at a girl's birthday party."

"True," said her other, better-liked friend, Bridget 'Bertha' Collins.

"Besides," Sandy added, "it's a daytime party. Everybody'll be gone by suppertime. Or at least I hope so!"

Richard strolled into the kitchen just then and made a beeline for the refrigerator. "Hello ladies," he said as he opened the refrigerator door without even looking at the women.

"Didn't you just eat, Rich?" asked Tracy.

"Just looking for a TV snack," he replied.

Just as Tracy was about to come back with a zinger, the telephone rang.

"I'll get it," said Richard. He closed the refrigerator door without taking anything out, and then stepped over to the phone, set on the kitchen counter. He clicked on the receiver button and brought the phone up to his ear. "Hello?" he said, and a second later, "Yes. She's here. May I ask who's calling?"

He paused, listening for a moment as the women looked on.

"What's this about?" he asked then.

"Who is it?" asked Sandy.

Richard put up a finger, wanting her to hold on a sec.

"Okay," he said into the phone. "She's right here."

Richard's suddenly serious expression sobered up the mood of the room. "It's the FBI, honey," he said then, stepping over to Sandy and handing her the phone. "They want to talk to you."

"*Shit*," exclaimed Tracy with a wide-eyed look at Sandy. "This is about Suzanne."

"Shush!" Bridget snapped at her.

Sandy put the phone to her ear. "Hello, this is Sandy."

The voice on the other end was that of an older woman, official sounding, but not stern.

"Sandy Whiting?"

"Yes, that's right."

"Mrs. Whiting, first I want to say that there's been no break or other updates on your sister's case, or your niece's. I'm calling you to let you know that couple of FBI special agents will be stopping by your home on either Friday or

Saturday, however, to talk to you about the case."

Sandy looked confused. "Is the FBI investigating their deaths?" she asked, never one to mince words when it came to what had happened to Suzanne and Becky. She knew, in her heart, they were both dead and not merely missing.

"We have a case file open on them, ma'am. We're working with the Massachusetts State Police."

"There's nothing new, though?" Sandy asked.

"I'm sorry, no. Not at this time. Special Agents Nicks and Fielding will be coming up to see you. They'll just want to go over some of the details of the case."

Just then, the two days the woman mentioned came to Sandy's mind. "My daughter's having a birthday party on Saturday afternoon."

"I see," said the woman. "They'll only be a few minutes, Mrs. Whiting. Maybe twenty or thirty minutes, at most. Is that okay?"

Sandy hesitated for a second before responding. "Yes— uh, yeah, that'll be fine, I guess."

"Very good, Mrs. Whiting. The agents will see you later this week then."

"Do I need to have any paperwork or anything?"

"No, ma'am. They'll just want to talk with you."

"Okay then. I'll be here."

Sandy held the phone to her ear for another moment, her mind preoccupied, as her friends and Richard watched her. She said into it, "Goodbye," and then set it on the kitchen table.

"It was about Suzy, wasn't it?" asked Tracy.

"Did they find something out?" Bridget asked.

Sandy shook her head. "No. No, nothing like that."

Richard placed his hands on Sandy's shoulders. "What'd they say?"

Sandy waved her hand in front of herself dismissively.

"They just want to talk to me about Suzy and Becky. I guess they're going over it with the state police."

"Well, that's got to be good news," Richard said.

"No," Sandy half-moaned. "They don't have anything new on the case. They're just coming by to go over what they already got."

"They're coming over here?" asked Bridget.

"Yeah," said Sandy. "On Friday or Saturday—the lady on the phone said she didn't know which day."

"*Saturday?*" squealed Tracy. "But that's Paula's birthday."

"It's all right," Sandy insisted.

"You want them showing up here on Paula's birthday," said Bridget, "and them getting you all upset with your daughter right here watching?"

Sandy turned to her and brought up her hands—*enough.* "It's been ten fucking years, Bridget," she fumed, "they're not going to say or do anything that I haven't long gotten over with by now."

Bridget started, "But it's her birth—"

"All right," Richard cut in, looking to come to Sandy's aid. "Let's not get all pissed off about this. Sandy's been talking about this for years, now. If she says she's good with them coming over, then that's it. Let it go."

Bridget rolled her eyes and put up her hands. "All right. I'll let it go."

Sandy came over to Bridget's side and placed a hand on her arm. "It's really okay, Bridget. I stopped crying about this a long time ago. I think I'm more angry at this point than anything." She smiled and winked at her. "Maybe you should hold me back when they get here, so I don't haul off and punch 'em."

Bridget laughed at that. "Sure, kiddo. I'll do that for you. Even though we all know they got it coming."

****

The clanking of the train car was the only noise breaking the journey's silence. Three days after Assistant Director Ledds assigned Special Agents Nicks and Fielding to the Massachusetts job, on this bright and warm Saturday morning, they were on their way up there.

Sam Nicks sat in a right window seat on Amtrak's 10:00 AM run to New Haven, Connecticut. Resting on his lap was his trusty Dell laptop, a cellular hotspot jacked into one of its USB adapters. He looked intently at the screen as he mulled a Google satellite map of the Hadley-Northampton, Massachusetts area. Sitting next to Nicks was Dan Fielding, his smartphone cradled in his lap while he texted his wife. Both men wore dark suits with white shirts. Nicks wore a thin red tie, while Fielding preferred a light blue one.

Fielding finished up messaging Kara and put away his phone. He looked at Nicks, glancing at his laptop, and then asked him, "Ain't Agent Weirdlee gonna to brief us when we get up there?"

Nicks answered without looking up. "Yeah. I just want to get a good layout of the land, though." He checked the time on the laptop's toolbar. "Weirdlee should have us set up by the time we get there. I'm going to call up the locals on the way up, too, and let them know we're on our way. We can stop in at the police station before we get into anything else and have a chat with the guys there."

Fielding kept his eyes on his partner's laptop. "How well you know this Weirdlee girl?"

Nicks looked at him. "I don't know her at all. Not personally. But she's worked with Ledds for about a year, now. Young woman, I think. Her specialty is mining intelligence. Somewhat of an odd sort, from what I hear, though."

Fielding glanced about the train car. "Ten-year-old cold case. Don't see why we're being called in on this one, partner. Just'a raisin' false hopes, is all I see."

Nicks returned his attention to his laptop. "Maybe."

Fielding looked at him. "I know you been with violent crimes for a while, now. You ever solve a case like this before?"

Nicks answered, surprisingly resolute. "Yes."

To that, Fielding pursed his lips and gave a nod. "Okay, then," he said. "I guess the boss called in the right man."

The train rattled on.

The two agents arrived in New Haven just after noontime. From there, they picked up a rental car—a dark red, late model Chevy Impala—for their drive north to Middlefield and their meeting with Sandy Whiting.

****

The Whiting clan and their friends had spent the better part of the morning getting ready to kick off Paula's backyard birthday party. The Whitings owned a raised ranch, with a garage housed on the right side ground floor. There was a small front yard, but a good-sized left side yard and a large back yard that included a garden and a large above-ground swimming pool. The whole outside was decorated for the special occasion, with balloons tied to trees and deck railings, and tables set up near the pool, each festooned with party favors and supplied with bowls of snacks. Sandy had also set up a couple of tables on the left side of the house, there for the adult attendees, and so allowing the kids to have their fun in the back. The spot also made for a convenient "watching" area to oversee who came in and who left the party. Already, over a dozen kids had arrived.

Presently, Sandy was sitting with her friends at one of the tables next to the house. Music emanated from a radio set at the center of the table, and as they chatted back and forth, classic rock filled the air. A large cooler, filled with their own stash of drinks, was set by their feet.

"If you don't have enough Sprite, Sandy, I can get some more at the store," Tracy offered.

Tracy, of course, was drinking the Sprite.

"I'll just shut you off after three," said Sandy, who herself remained in early morning coffee mode with a cup in front of her.

Bridget, meanwhile, had started up on her wine coolers. She sat with her feet up on a spare chair, lounging comfortably.

"So, them guys never stop by yesterday to see you?" Tracy asked Sandy.

"The FBI guys? No. They'll probably come by today."

Bridgett took a swig from her wine cooler. "I wonder what they want? They gotta have something."

Sandy shook her head. "The lady the other day said they didn't. They just wanted to review it—or something like that."

"Picked a stupid day for it," said Tracy. "Coming here, I mean."

Sandy shook her head and sighed. "It doesn't matter. I am *long* over all that emotional bullshit."

"Fuck ups," quipped Tracy. "They should have had Columbo on it. He would have nailed that asshole."

"I never liked that show," said Bridgett. "Always thought he was a perv."

They all laughed at that.

Like a clarion call then, the song "I Love Rock and Roll"

started up, and the women all thumped the table in keeping a beat to it. Bridgett sang along.

"Is Larry coming over?" Sandy asked Tracy of her husband.

Tracy shook her head vigorously. "No way. He said he's got yard work to do—which means about an hour of work and four hours sitting on his ass watching TV."

"I hear that," Sandy said.

Bridgett gave up on singing and took another drink from her wine cooler. She smacked her lips and eyed the bottle happily. "Gonna run outta these quick."

Just then, Richard, dressed in a tee shirt and shorts, came out of the house and walked over to the women. Tracy called out to him in greeting, and he looked at her and Bridget, nodding to them, "Girls," before getting behind Sandy and putting his hands on her shoulders. He leaned his head down close to hers. "FBI is on the way up, hon," he said quietly in her ear. "Said they'll be here in about twenty or thirty minutes."

"Shit," Tracy swore.

"Here we go," said Bridgett.

Richard crouched by Sandy's side. "You gonna be okay?"

She frowned at him, saying, "I'm fine, Richard," before looking to her friends. "Guys, I appreciate you all being so protective, but really, it's been ten years. I did all my crying a long time ago. I don't think there's anything they could say that would bring it all back—not the way I felt back then."

"I wonder what they want, though," Bridgett persisted.

Richard stood up straight again and sighed. "Ah, hell," he said, putting his hands in his pockets, "probably just somebody looking for a promotion and wants to say he looked into this thing."

Sandy laughed uneasily. "Yeah."

Another car showed up with more kids in it, and they all piled out and walked across the side lawn on their way to the backyard festivities. A few minutes later, Paula came around from the back to see her mom and dad. She clutched her iPhone in her hand.

"Mom, Dad," she said. "Ricky wants to come over today. That's okay, right?"

Sandy looked back at her, then turned her eyes to Richard, awaiting his reply.

Richard frowned jokingly at his daughter. "What's he want to come to a girls' party for?"

Paula rolled her eyes and shrugged. "Uh, because there's *girls* here?"

"Who's he bringing along?" Sandy asked suspiciously.

"No one," Paula answered. "Just him."

Richard pointed to the ground. "He stays here, in this yard. And so do you."

Paula moaned, "I know."

Sandy nodded to her. "All right, then."

Paula's face brightened and she smiled. "Thanks!" She spun around and made for the backyard while slapping her phone to her ear and chattering away.

"So much for a girls' party," quipped Tracy.

"One guy," Sandy to her, straight-faced.

"I'm gonna bring out the dogs and burgers for the grill," said Richard, starting to walk away.

"Have fun, chef," Sandy said with a smile.

"Let me know when the Feds get here," he said back to her.

"Oh, you'll know," she replied.

Bridgett polished off her wine cooler and reached into the cooler for another. "Where we putting the empties?" she asked, glancing around.

Sandy answered, "Just leave them on the table and I'll

collect 'em later."

"A hotdog sounds good right about now," said Tracy.

"Get one for me while your back there," Sandy said, volunteering her friend for a food run.

"Yeah," added Bridget. "I like mine with mustard and relish."

Tracy frowned at her. "What am I, a waitress?"

She got up anyway, though. "Everybody gets mustard, only."

Off she went then to fetch the dogs.

Sandy and Bridgett bantered on some more about how many other kids they expected and what to do if more boys showed up. Then, as if on cue, young Ricky pulled up on his bright green moped—not the most macho of vehicles to arrive on.

"Out back," Sandy pointed as he walked by them.

"Hi Mrs. Whiting," he said.

Tracy returned with the dogs and some napkins, and the women settled in for their little snack. The banter continued.

Finishing up afterward, Sandy wiped her mouth with a napkin and took a drink from the last of her coffee. "Time for a soda, I think," she said. She opened up the cooler and sifted through the cans of soda there. Spotting a Coke, she picked it out and popped it open.

The radio played on. Next up came Cyndi Lauper's "Girls Just Wanna Have Fun." Tracy laughed and clapped to it, recalling when the song came out in the 1980s. Sandy smiled, too, rocking in her seat to the rhythm of the music.

Bridgett looked off to the street then, and so was the first to spot the red Impala pulling up to the house.

"Shit," she said. "I think that's them."

Sandy immediately stopped her groove, and Tracy did the same.

None of the women said another word to each other as two well-dressed men got out of the car. The driver—a tall, thin man with a serious look about him—removed his sunglasses and tucked them into his jacket's breast pocket as he looked to the ladies and started off towards them. The other man with him—about average in height and appearing more at ease—joined him.

Sandy slowly stood up from her chair. Her eyes locked on the taller man as he walked ahead with his partner.

Wafting in the air the whole time, "Girls Just Wanna Have Fun" played on...

Some boys take a beautiful girl
and hide her away from the rest of the world...

Sandy, though, couldn't hear a thing. For everything from the past had suddenly come back to her. All of the anguish and the despair, all of the hopelessness and the heartbreaking loss, and the frustrations and endless pain— everything she had endured for so many months and years after her sister and niece were so cruelly taken away from her, had returned. And she broke into tears as the agents approached her. She cried like she hadn't cried in ten long, lonely years. She cried like everything had happened just yesterday, and everything—every bit of it—was happening to her, all over again.

3

Agent Weirdlee

The door to the scrappy little Northampton bar opened, and in walked an attractive woman, sharply dressed in a white blouse, black skirt, and a pair of black, knee-high buckled boots. She wore a black shawl draped over her shoulders, and her long, dark red hair fell neatly behind her. A small, stylish purse hung from her left shoulder. The woman's slender shape and smooth, tanned legs caught the eyes of quite a few of the male patrons there as she made her way along the bar. She took a seat at its far end, nearest the bartender's register.

"Hi," greeted a customer sitting just to her left. He was a gruff and unshaven sort, older-looking, with a chunky build to him. He wore a pair of well-worn blue jeans and a wrinkled long-sleeved shirt, and clutched a bottle of Bud Light in his hand, nursing it every so often in quick fashion.

The woman smiled back at him, appearing not at all bothered by his rough looks. "Good afternoon," she said to him as she set her purse on the bar. She glanced away then, seeking the attention of the young female bartender.

The bartender had seen her enter and then watched her take her seat. After finishing up with her current customer, she strolled over to the new arrival.

"What can I get for you?" she asked her.

The woman pursed her lips, considering, and then answered, "Oh, a whisky sour."

"Short glass?"

The woman nodded. "Sure. On the rocks, with a slice of lemon, please."

The bartender stepped away to get her drink.

The gruff looking man to her left spoke up again. "How's it going?" he asked her with an innocent smile.

She looked back at him and smiled as before. "I'm doing fine. Thank you."

The man detected an accent to her voice—as if she'd come from the eastern part of the state.

"You from Boston or somethin', maybe?"

"Hmm..." the woman considered. "I'm not from around here, anyway."

The man chuckled lazily. "Oh, you're a mystery woman, then."

She batted her eyebrows at him without saying anything, then turned to face the bar again, paying him no more mind.

The man kept his smile as he watched her there. Then, thinking better of it, he decided not to push himself on her, and so turned his attention back to his own drink as the bartender arrived with hers.

The woman looked at the bartender. "Get a lot of after-work clientele, do you?"

The bartender frowned and replied, "We have our regulars, like most places." Then she eyed the man sitting next to the woman. "Some work, some don't."

The woman took her drink delicately in her hand and swirled the little ice cubes around. "I imagine they come in shifts, like most."

"Yeah, kinda, I guess," the bartender replied. "That'll be seven-fifty."

The woman reached into her purse and pulled out a small black billfold. Opening it, she slipped out a twenty-dollar bill.

The bartender, watching her, noticed something else in the billfold, too: an identification card that read *FBI*. She flashed her eyebrows and said loudly, "FBI?"

All around the bar, faces turned to look at them.

The woman replied calmly, "Yes," and took a sip from her drink.

"Wow," said the bartender with a smile. "That's cool."

The gruff-looking man craned his head back to look at the woman again, giving her a very noticeable once-over.

"Sheeet..." he said. "FBI?"

The woman looked back at him out of the corner of her eye. "Mhmm."

"You working?" asked the bartender.

The woman shook her head. "No. Not today, really."

The man kept ogling her. "They sure make 'em pretty in the FBI these days."

The woman smirked at that, then turned her attention back to the bartender. She asked her while sliding forward the twenty-dollar bill, "Day shift workers come in around dinner time, night shifters after eleven?"

The bartender fetched up the bill, then turned to look at small a clock behind the bar. It read 1:41 PM.

"Yeah," she said. "They start coming in around four or five o'clock." She went to the register then to fetch the woman's change.

The gruff man, meanwhile, settled himself in and kept his eyes on the pretty FBI girl.

"What's your name?" he asked her. "Mine's Fred."

She looked at him out of the corner of her eye again. "Special Agent Weirdlee," she said to him. Then she turned in her chair to look at him squarely, and it was then that she first sensed a rather innocent, simpleminded nature to his expression—as if some manner of disability affected his mind. "Joanna Weirdlee," she offered with a smile. "And you can call me Joanna."

He smiled in turn. "Nice to meet ya, Joanna."

She nodded back. "You a regular here, Fred?"

The bartender returned with the agent's change, setting it on the bar. "He's a regular, all right," she said in a smarmy tone. "A regular pain in the ass."

"Aww," said Fred. "She's lyin'. I'm a *real* nice guy. Really."

Weirdlee, of course, was familiar with the sarcastic camaraderie of neighborhood bars. "I bet you are, too," she said to him.

"Fred's all right," the bartender offered jovially as she walked away to serve another customer.

Off by the rear of the pub, a young man strolled over to the jukebox there and slipped a five-dollar bill into the feeder. As he tapped in his selections, his first choice, Nirvana's "About a Girl," began to play.

"So," Fred said eagerly to Weirdlee, slapping his hands together and rubbing them. "Whatcha working on these days? Somethin' around here?"

Weirdlee took another sip of her drink, taking her time. "You know a lot of the regulars around here, do you, Fred?" she asked him, ignoring his own inquiry.

Fred looked around the place. "Yeah, I guess so."

Weirdlee reached into her purse again, and from it she slid out her Android smartphone. She tapped on it a few times, then swiped through a couple of images. Finding what she was looking for, she turned the phone to show it to Fred.

"How about this man?" she asked him. "You know him?"

Fred looked at the image. The man in it was older—about in his mid-fifties, with a thin, drawn face, and deeply set brown eyes. His hair was short and tousled. The image, Fred noticed, was obviously a police mug shot. And he recognized the man right away.

"Yeah," he said. "That's Johnny. He comes in here pretty regular." He looked at Weirdlee. "You lookin' for him?"

Weirdlee drew her phone back and tapped off the display. She tucked the phone back into her purse as she answered, "No, not actually."

Fred appeared puzzled. "Why you got his picture, then?"

Weirdly gave him a guarded look, feigning seriousness. "Oh, I think that's a private matter, Fred." She took another sip of her whiskey sour. Then, keeping her eyes on her glass, she asked him, "He comes by here on weekends, too, Fred? Saturday nights? Like tonight?"

Fred took in a long drink from his beer before answering. "Yeah. You wanna meet him?"

Weirdlee glanced about the room. "Oh..." she said, taking a sip from her drink. "Maybe someday. Not tonight, though."

She stood up from her seat then and gathered up her change, leaving two dollars for the bartender.

Fred seemed disappointed. "You leaving?"

She gave him a nod as she slung her purse strap over her shoulder. "Late lunch," she said. "You know any good restaurants around here?"

Fred smiled. "Sure. Fitzgerald's is right down road, here, going right and around the corner. We got Maximilian's just across the street from here, too."

Weirdlee looked out the window facing the street, where the afternoon sun shone brightly. "Okay."

Another man sitting nearby, who'd been eavesdropping on the conversation, offered his own recommendation. "They got food here, too, you know. It's okay."

Still another guy at the far end of the bar offered his, as well. "Benson's got good burgers. It's a good walk from here, though."

Weirdlee smiled at the both of them as she started out. "All right, then. Choices."

"See ya later, FBI girl," said Fred, having already forgotten her name.

She tossed him a wave as she strolled to the door. "Bye-bye, Fred."

She departed then, leaving behind a clutch of ogling men.

"Damn," said the man at the far end of the bar, shaking his head. "That was *smokin'* hot."

The bartender laughed. "She is *waaay* out of your leagues, guys."

Fred smiled back at her, smug in his own right. "Yeah, but she remembered my name," he beamed. Then he looked over at the door, his stilted imagination already undressing the lovely FBI agent.

He couldn't wait to tell John all about her.

****

Agent Weirdlee hopped into her rental car, a yellow Ford Focus, and drove north along Pleasant Street for a couple of blocks before arriving at the Hotel Northampton, where she'd already gotten a room for herself and reserved another for her fellow agents coming up from Middlefield.

After finding a place to park in the back lot, she went into the hotel. Her smartphone buzzed as she strolled through the lobby. She stopped and reached into her purse, pulling it out. Looking at a new text message alert, she smiled and tapped on it.

The new message read, *Status check.*

She thumb-typed her response: *Rooms set. Need to eat. See you tonight?*

Message back to her: *Did you do an intro?*

Her reply: *Word is out.*

And the response: *Good. Yes. Maybe dinnertime.*

It's a date, she replied.

C u soon, came the other.

k, she ended.

She tapped off the phone and pushed it back into her purse. She sighed, glancing about, and continued on her way.

Lunch, for today, would be in the hotel's cafe.

****

John Henneger strode into O'Brien's Pub and made for his usual spot at the bar, just off to the far-left side. Henneger was a tall and lanky guy, his face much like his mug shot. He wore jeans and a black t-shirt on this late afternoon, both filthy from a day's working construction. Others there eyeballed him as he walked along, and as he settled onto his usual barstool, he noticed another regular there, Fred Duncan, looking at him with a wide smile.

"You're in trouble, Johnny," Fred teased him.

Henneger scowled at him. "What?"

The bartender walked up to where Henneger sat. With a bottle of Budweiser in hand, she popped it open and set it on the bar in front of him.

"FBI, John," she said to him. "What the fuck have you been up to?"

Fred slapped the bar in frustration. "Aww!" he howled, "I wanted to tell him!"

"What the fuck are you guys talking about?" Henneger shot back, eyeing them both.

Fred opened up: "A real nice lookin' girl came in here today. FBI girl. She showed me a picture of you and asked if I knew you."

Henneger leered at him. "What the fuck did she want?"

Fred shrugged. "She didn't say."

Henneger glanced around the room, suddenly aware that he was the center of attention. He looked back at Fred. "She comin' back here?"

"I dunno," said Fred. "She didn't say."

Henneger got up from his seat and walked over to where Fred sat at the bar. He asked him in a lowered tone, "What'd you tell her about me?"

"Didn't tell her nothin'," said Fred. "She didn't ask me nothin'—'cept to ask if you came in here a lot."

Henneger gave him a hard swat on his shoulder. "And what'd you say?"

Shaken by Henneger's reaction, Fred answered nervously, "Just that you came by here every so often."

Henneger nodded slowly, leering at him. "Yeah, well, you got a big fuckin' mouth, asshole."

"I-I didn't say nothin'," Fred stammered.

"Hey, John, relax," said the bartender. "The chick was a pop tart. She was only in here for a couple minutes. Didn't even finish her drink."

Henneger kept his glare on Fred before turning to the bartender. "Fuckin' shit," he grumbled.

He walked back over to his barstool then and stayed standing as he grabbed his bottle of beer and chugged down a hefty gulp.

Fred turned back to his own beer on the bar, his mood suddenly changed from being merry to noticeably rattled. He was, much as Weirdlee had sensed, a man already handicapped by an injured mind. Trouble of any sort, then, was enough to choke him up terribly.

Henneger glared at the bartender, then jabbed his finger on the bar. "She comes back in here while I'm away, you tell her I wanna see her."

The bartender raised an eyebrow and smiled. "Oh, I'll be sure and tell her that, John."

Henneger took another swig from his beer. "Fuckin' bitch."

He'd show her who she was dealing with.

4

The Scene of the Crime

Nicks and Fielding sat at a small conference table across from Hadley Police Chief Victor Towers and one of his officers, Sergeant Jim Banning. Ten years prior, Banning had been, in addition to the first cop at the scene, also one of cops assigned to investigate the disappearance of Suzanne and Becky Kerch. The sergeant brought along with him whatever files he had from the investigation. The chief, meanwhile, sat in front of a laptop computer with the department's complete crime file on the investigation opened up there for reference.

"So, the Feds are finally looking into this after ten years, are they?" said Banning, eyeing the two agents with an air of mistrust. He rapped his files on the table in front of him. "A little late on the timing, I'd say."

Nicks sat back in his chair, entirely unimpressed with the local officer's sarcasm.

"Better late than never," he said to him. "You know how that is, right?"

Towers looked at the two men and cleared his throat to break the tension. "All right, then," he said, "let's get started." He glanced at his laptop before looking to Nicks and Fielding. "Now, you two gentlemen are looking into this investigation as a cold case, I'm sure. But I can tell you, we never closed this one, and we never put it to rest. This is still an active case in our files, and we're still looking into leads to this very day."

"You have fresh leads?" Nicks asked.

Towers frowned. "Figure of speech."

Banning tossed his files onto the table. "Look, we've investigated this case from every possible angle there is. You think we don't wanna arrest that scumbag, Henneger? We know them girls didn't go off on some trip somewhere."

"Where did you think they went off to, then, when they went missing?" Nicks asked.

Banning sneered at him. "What?"

Nicks looked at Fielding, and then back at Banning. "What was it—that following Wednesday when you called up Henneger, asking him about the women?"

Banning shrugged. "I don't know. Was it a Wednesday? It was at night, I know that, after the woman's boss called us."

Fielding nodded. "That would be the Wednesday after they went missing."

"Yeah, so what?" Banning said.

"Were you guys busy or something?" Nicks asked.

"What are you talking about?" Banning replied. "Don't you judge us, mister. You weren't there. I went out there myself that morning. There wasn't anything going on. Shit, you know how many calls we get like that? We can't just go around searching people's properties after every call."

"How many calls *do* you get like that, Sergeant?" Fielding asked.

"Look," Towers intervened. "We're not here to fuss over who did what wrong."

"You're right," said Nicks. "And my partner and I aren't here to listen to some guy worried about us pissing on his lawn." He looked at Banning. "Maybe if you did your job right the first time around, we wouldn't be out here having to bother you."

"That's enough," Towers said, pointing at Nicks. "I don't like that accusation."

"Those girls were dead!" Banning howled. "And nothing we did back then was gonna bring 'em back."

Fielding put up a hand. "Maybe we should take a timeout."

"Listen," Towers said. He rapped his knuckles on his laptop. "We've got all our case files right here. And you've got Banning's personal notes, here, too."

"If you can read my handwriting," Banning added.

Nicks looked from Banning to the chief. "I've already read your department files, Chief. I'd like to go check out Henneger's place, where the girls went missing, if we can."

"He don't live there anymore," Banning said.

"I know," said Nicks. "They didn't move the house, did they?"

Towers crumpled back in his chair and sighed. "The people living there now have been through this before. I guess we might as well get it over with."

Banning got up from his seat, his personal files clutched in his hands. "That place is as clean as a whistle. It's been ten years. You're wasting your time."

The two agents got up from their chairs.

"Wouldn't be the first time," Nicks quipped. "Won't be the last."

****

Nicks drove the agents' car on the ride out to Henneger's old home, following behind the chief's squad car. Fielding, sitting in the passenger's seat next to Nicks, watched the scenery pass by outside. The younger agent then looked over at his partner, his curiosity piqued.

"You really mean what ya said back there?" he asked, his southern accent coming through.

Nicks glanced at him. "Mean what?"

"You know—about them not doing their job."

Nicks kept his eyes on the road ahead of them. He thought about Fielding's question.

"Let me tell you," he said. "A lot of people go missing because they want to go missing. But then you've got other folks who disappear because of foul play. And man, when that happens, you've gotta move your ass. The first seventy-two hours are critical. You play drag-ass, you're missing your window."

Fielding tried to figure out his partner's thinking. "You sayin' you think them girls might'a been still alive after Sunday?"

Nicks shook his head. "No. Those women were killed Saturday night or Sunday morning, I'm pretty sure. But our suspect didn't necessarily get rid of the bodies right away. He had to put them somewhere, you know?"

Fielding nodded. "Yeah." He turned his head back to the window, looking outside again. "Still, the police didn't know anything until that boss called. And they did have a car go out there."

"Read the file, partner. The boss told the cops that Suzanne Kerch had been out since that Monday. And the kid is gone, too? Fuck..."

Fielding looked back at him. "You think they shoulda searched the property that day? What—Wednesday?"

Nicks glanced at his partner. "What do you think Henneger was doing all week?"

Fielding shrugged. "I dunno. Working?"

Nicks shook his head. "The neighbors said he packed his van three times with junk that week."

"Yeah," said Fielding, "but they searched the dump afterward and didn't find anything."

Nicks let out a cynical laugh. "They checked a few dumps, actually. But just because a guy hauls out a load of junk doesn't mean he's taking it to a dump. He could have taken a ride anywhere."

Fielding looked out the window again, his eyes darting about the scenery. "I suppose so."

The agents tailed the chief's car, traveling west along Route 9 before taking a left onto West Street. Driving to the end of that road, they turned left onto Bay Road. From there, it was just a short drive up the street to get to Henneger's former home, set on the left side, or south side, of Bay.

The house—a sixty-five-year-old white, two-story colonial with black shutters—had a dirt driveway on its left side that led up to a detached garage. Behind the house, just beyond the property's back lawn, a narrow growth of trees extended in either direction, forming a natural border between all the backyards that lined Bay Road and a large, tilled field beyond.

The chief pulled his cruiser into the driveway and parked behind a dark red Ford Explorer. The agents made a u-turn and parked on the street curb, directly in front of the house. They all got out of their cars then and made for the front door.

The door opened before they could get there and a blonde woman, looking to be in her mid-forties and wearing jean shorts and a white halter top, stood in the doorway. The chief had called ahead, of course, so they were expected.

"Hi," she said. "Back again, huh?"

The police had talked with the current homeowners a couple of times before in previous years, so this was starting to get routine for both parties. Tiresome, but routine.

"Afternoon, Mrs. Benardez," Towers greeted her. He pointed off to the FBI agents following behind him. "These are the guys I told you about on the phone."

The woman eyed Nicks and Fielding as they walked up to the door. "FBI, huh?"

"Yes, ma'am," said Nicks. He glanced about the place. "You've lived here a few years, now, Mrs. Benardez?"

"About five years," she answered.

He looked at her directly. "Would it be okay for us to come inside and maybe get a quick tour from you?"

Mrs. Benardez shrugged, seeming bored by the idea. "Why not?" she replied, eyeballing the chief. "I've got it down pat, by now."

She stepped aside and let them in.

Inside the place, the visitors found themselves in a hallway. Off to their right was the living room, while directly in front of them was a stairwell that led up to the second floor. The kitchen was off to their left.

"Where first?" Mrs. Benardez asked.

Chief Towers turned to the agents. He pointed here and there as he briefed them. "The kitchen has a pantry on the other end, and also a bathroom. The living room, there, has a dining room on its far end, facing the backyard." He pointed down the hallway leading to the stairwell. "There's a staircase leading down to the cellar at the end of the hall, here. You can see the door under the stairs going up."

Nicks gave him a nod, seeing the basement door under the stairway. "Let's start with the ground floor," he said. "Then we can go upstairs. We'll check out the basement last."

That agreed to, Mrs. Benardez began her tour.

This was a straightforward affair, with little talking going on as the party passed from one area of the house to the next. The agents, after all, weren't actually searching for anything. They just wanted to see what the house looked like on the inside. Every so often, Nicks would ask Benardez or the chief if this or that room was the same as it was when Henneger sold the place. The answer was "yes" in all but one instance, where the chief pointed out that the dining room had once been separate from the living room, but the Benardezes tore down the interior wall to open up that part of the house. Mrs. Benardez showed them the master bedroom upstairs that had once been Henneger's and Suzanne Kerch's, and, across the hall, Becky Kerch's bedroom. Once finished with the upstairs tour, the group went down to the basement. There, Mrs. Benardez showed the agents the unfinished laundry room area—currently strewn with sheets and a pile of clothes—and, at the far side, she pointed out the oil tank and furnace area.

Still standing near the laundry area, Nicks looked up at the ceiling, then glanced all around the basement.

"The laundry machines were down here when Henneger lived here, too?" he asked Towers.

Towers nodded. "Yeah."

"These are ours, though," Mrs. Benardez clarified, pointing at the washer and dryer. "He took his with him."

"Right," said Nicks. He looked at Towers and Fielding. "The police report said Suzanne talked to a friend on the phone the same night that she and her daughter disappeared—about nine o'clock, was it? Suzanne mentioned during the phone call that her daughter was doing laundry."

"Yeah," said Towers. "Musta been down here."

"You know," said Mrs. Benardez, "if we had known people got killed here, we never would have bought the place."

"Missing," Fielding corrected her.

"Whatever," she said. "I get the creeps just thinking about it."

Nicks looked at Towers and Mrs. Benardez. "Can you

two do me a favor?" he asked them.

"What's that?" Towers replied.

"Can you go up to the second floor for me? Start in the hallway up there, first, and just yell at each other. Then go into the master bedroom and do it again."

"*What?*" Mrs. Benardez asked.

Fielding nodded, understanding what Nicks wanted to do. "We just want to see if we can hear you guys arguing from down here."

"Yeah, right," said Towers.

The two headed upstairs then.

Nicks walked over to the washer and dryer. He fired up the washer, then grabbed some clothes from the nearby clothes pile and threw them into the dryer. He started that up, too.

A moment later, the yelling began. Both agents could hear the shouting pretty well from where they were. After a few more seconds then, the yelling dampened to nothing at all, and the two men assumed that the chief and Mrs. Benardez had moved into the bedroom.

"What are ya thinkin'?" Fielding asked Nicks. "Even if the girl heard 'em arguing, not sure that would mean anything."

Nicks drummed his fingers on the dryer. "I don't know..." he said thoughtfully. "Maybe a timing thing."

"Timing?"

Nicks eyed him. "Hard to take down two people at once. But if the girl was used to them fighting, she might have just stayed down here, thinking she'd wait it out. And if Henneger did kill the mother upstairs first, then he'd have to take care of things with the daughter. Can't just let her go."

Fielding cringed at the gruesome scenario that conjured up in his mind. "He'd just come down here and kill that girl in cold blood, ya think?"

Nicks gave him a nod as he turned off both the washer and dryer. "Might have felt he had no choice. Not unless he wanted to go to prison right off."

Fielding shook his head. "That's a hell of thing..."

The chief and Mrs. Benardez started down the stairs.

"Well?" asked Towers, coming up to them. "What'd you hear?"

Nicks replied with a question of his own. "You two yelled in the hallway first and then in the bedroom?"

"That's right."

"All right," said Nicks. "We heard you in the hallway well enough. Nothing after you moved into the bedroom."

The chief looked around, then up at the ceiling overhead. "We figured the girl—whether she was down here or in the kitchen or wherever—heard the two arguing, and she ran up to help out her mom. That's when all hell coulda broke loose."

Nicks gave a nod to that. "Yeah. That's possible. Or he came down here to get her. The neighbors never heard anything, though, huh?"

The chief put his hands on his hips and shook his head. "Nope." Then he batted his head upwards. "The state forensics guys pulled up a bunch of floorboards, too— second floor hallway, Henneger's bedroom, and down in the living room and dining room—checking for trace blood."

"Nothing?" asked Nicks.

"Nothin'."

"Holy shit." Mrs. Benardez shuttered. "This is too much for me." She started back up the stairs. "You guys let me know when you're done here."

Nicks asked her, "Mrs. Benardez, do you mind if we take a walk around your backyard before we go?"

"Go ahead," she said with a wave of her hand as she walked up the stairs.

Outside, Nicks and Fielding strolled around the backyard on their own, eventually coming to the edge of the narrow wooded area bordering the yard. From there, they could see that the woods overlooked a small, swampy gully that ran all along the wooded area's length. The gully was actually an overflow from the Connecticut River, which lay about a quarter of a mile away on the other side of a sparsely settled residential road at the far end of the tilled field beyond the gully.

Fielding looked into the gully. "I suppose they searched through all this shit, aye?"

"No doubt," said Nicks. He peered off across the field then, where he could see the road fronting the river. "You read anything about Henneger owning a boat?"

Fielding shrugged. "Don't recall."

"We'll have to check," Nicks said. "They dragged the river all around here and then downstream some. I can't picture him, though, dumping their bodies there. Too damn risky." He turned to Fielding. "This guy's pretty smart. If he did kill those two women, he did a better job of covering his tracks than just dumping them in a river."

Fielding shook his head at the thought, considering, once more, the murderous scenario Nicks had suggested earlier. "You know," he said, "it's one thing to kill someone in the heat of passion or anger. But to actually go downstairs...and kill that poor girl in cold blood. I can't imagine."

Nicks looked thoughtfully at his partner. He wondered how much he'd seen in his short career with the agency. Fielding was a white collar, cyber crimes guy before coming over to him. Had he even seen a dead body before?

"It happens a lot more than you think," he said to him then. "It's just something you have to consider. You have to think like they do—put yourself in their shoes."

Fielding gave him a pained look. "Put yourself in *their* shoes?"

"That's right," said Nicks. He looked back towards the house, behind them. "Not everyone makes mistakes, you know. You can't just sit around waiting for them to make that one screw up that breaks your case. Sometimes you have to ask yourself, 'What would I do if I killed two people and I had to get rid of their bodies?'"

Fielding muttered, "Can't imagine such a thing."

Nicks looked at him and answered his own question matter-of-factly.

"Stash 'em where nobody'd look."

5

Dinner for Three

Joanna Weirdlee chose a table set against the far wall at the Hotel Northampton's Wiggins Tavern. She'd already started on a glass of red wine. Beside her glass, too, were set two black folders. The table itself had three menus placed around it—one in front of Weirdlee, and the other two set to either side.

Located in a lower part of the hotel, the tavern was a small, dimly lit place, with a low ceiling and a rustic feel to its decor. Presently, besides Weirdlee, there were just a few other patrons sitting at some other tables.

Agents Nicks and Fielding descended the few steps leading into the tavern, having first checked into their room and dropped off their baggage there. Coming to a small serving bar, Nicks led Fielding around it to get to the main dining area beyond. Nicks spied the pretty redhead from across the way. He gave her a look, and she spotted him and tossed a wave back.

"That's our girl," he said to Fielding.

The two men approached Weirdlee's table.

"Special Agent Weirdlee, I presume," Nicks greeted her.

She smiled back. "At your service, Agent Nicks," she said, recognizing him from his file photo. Her Boston accent flared as she spoke. She looked at Fielding. "And Agent Fielding. A pleasure."

"Mind if we join you?" Nicks asked, offering the formality of a request.

"I've already got your menus," she replied. "The waitress

will be back in a bit."

The two men took their seats to either side of Weirdlee. As they settled in, she picked up the folders in front of her and set one each before the agents. "These are for you," she said.

"Ah, gifts," quipped Nicks.

The waitress had spotted the two men joining Weirdlee, and she approached the table.

"Can I get you some drinks?" she asked them.

"Coffee and an ice water," said Nicks.

"Cream and sugar?" she asked.

"One sugar and milk," he replied.

"Sure."

She turned to Fielding. "And you, sir?"

Fielding eyeballed Weirdlee's wine before making his choice. "I guess a glass of wine, red, will do. Can I get a glass of water, too?"

"Sure," she answered. "I'll be right back with your drinks."

The waitress walked off.

Nicks picked up the menu and opened it. "Shall we eat first and talk business later, or do both at the same time?"

"We can do both," said Weirdlee. "I've had a long day. I'd like to go to bed early tonight."

"Right."

Weirdlee got into it then.

"The two folders have some background info on some people of interest I've gathered up. I also have some photos I took of the area, and I put a lot of those in a shared Dropbox folder online. I've shared them with each of your emails."

Nicks reached for his phone and fired it up. He checked his email as Weirdlee continued.

"I've visited with the Northampton police already. I

asked them about Henneger, since he lives here now. They said he's been clean since he moved here after getting out of jail for his drug stint." Then she remembered, "By the way, this hotel is perfectly situated. The cops and the courthouse are just behind us, here, and the registry of deeds and probate is across the street in front. Couldn't get any more convenient than that."

Nicks nodded in agreement.

Fielding opened his folder and browsed through the paperwork inside. This included some computer-printed photos, one of which was of Henneger's new home in Northampton. He'd purchased a small, dark blue, wood-sided ranch style house on Riverside Drive in the city.

"How'd this come about, here?" he asked. "Did he lose his house in Hadley when he went to prison?"

Weirdlee shook her head. "He picked up a renter before he went away. Some woman he knew. He had the place put on the market for a couple years, but it didn't sell until about a year after he got out."

"That's kinda weird," Fielding quipped. He grinned at Weirdlee and winked. "No pun intended." Then he looked again at the photo of Henneger's house. "If he was gonna move, you'd think he'd wanna get the hell outta Dodge—I mean *way* out. Like to another part of the country."

"Maybe he just got tired of the view," said Weirdlee.

"Or maybe too many bad memories," offered Nicks in a more sober tone. He was working with his phone, still, going through the photos Weirdlee had put on Dropbox.

The waitress arrived with the men's drinks. She set them before the agents.

"Are you ready to order?" she asked them all.

"I already know what I'm getting," said Weirdlee. "Cup of clam chowder and a side Caesar salad."

"I haven't even looked at the menu yet," Fielding said.

Nicks picked up his menu and checked out the appetizers. "I'll take the....sea scallops, and a cup of, let's see...French onion soup."

The waitress nodded, jotting down his order, and then turned to Fielding. "You, sir?"

Fielding felt hurried as he browsed the selections. "Uhh..." he started, "how about...umm, uhh...just the chicken pot pie, I guess. Jeez."

"Okay," the waitress said. "Anything else for anyone? Appetizers?"

"Nope," said Nicks.

"We're good," said Weirdlee, smiling.

"Okay. I'll be right out with your dinner then."

She stepped away, and the agents continued with their conversation.

"So, I stopped in at one of Henneger's regular haunts earlier today," Weirdlee said. "The man gets around, I have to say. A regular bar hound."

"People get to know you?" Nicks asked.

Weirdlee took a sip of her wine. She smiled at Nicks. "I'm the FBI girl," she said sweetly. "Talk of the town."

"Good," said Nicks. "Henneger should know by now."

"We gotta talk with him, right?" Fielding asked.

Nicks nodded. "Yeah. Maybe during the week sometime. Let's let him stew for a bit. I don't want to catch him when he's drinking, either. He'll probably be a little uptight when he sees us."

"I could talk to him," offered Weirdlee.

"You might do that," said Nicks. "But later. I want to make it clear to him that you're not alone up here."

Weirdlee batted her eyelashes. "Why, Sheriff, how gentlemanly of you."

Nicks smirked at her. "Precaution."

Fielding, however, appeared puzzled by the matter.

"Later? You mean Agent Weirdlee's stayin' on here?"

"Yeah," said Nicks. "We're a threesome on this outing."

"Oh," Fielding replied. "I thought she was just our advance setup." He looked at her directly. "No offense."

"None taken," she said.

The agents talked some more then, and soon afterward their dinners arrived. Little was said as they ate their meals. After they finished up, the waitress stopped by again to clear their plates.

"Well," said Weirdlee to her colleagues, "I think I'm going to call it a night."

"It was nice to finally meet you," said Nicks.

"Yes," added Fielding. "Same here."

"Nice meeting you both," Weirdlee said as she got up from her seat. She fetched her purse, which was wrapped around her chair's rung. "See you in the morning?"

"Maybe," said Nicks. "I'm going to walk around town early, stretch the legs."

"Fair enough," she said. "Good night."

Weirdlee walked off then and left the tavern.

Fielding looked at Nicks and smiled. "She stuck us with the tab, I see."

Nicks grinned back at him. "On the company."

Fielding gave a nod, then looked back towards the tavern's entrance, through which Weirdlee had left. "She's a good looker," he said, "but you know what they say about redheads." He turned back to Nicks. "A little psycho."

Nicks downed the last of his water, then said, "She not a real redhead."

Fielding let out a laugh. "What? How do you know that?"

Nicks reached for his wallet, pulling it out of his back pocket.

"Redheads don't tan very well, Special Agent," he said.

Then he raised an eyebrow. "And that lady's got one hell of a tan."

6

Sunday

Nicks was up early and out of the hotel by just after sunrise. He had a lot of thinking to do as he took his morning stroll around Northampton's bisecting streets and ways. First, he headed south down King Street to get to Main Street. Taking a right from there, he made his way to Center Street and followed that road north, past the Northampton Police Station. He decided not to pay them a visit just yet, and instead kept walking.

He mulled over the case as he went along. He'd taken notes when he and Fielding had met with Suzanne Kerch's sister, Sandy, down in Connecticut. The woman was quite emotional at first, but managed to settle down as they talked. She'd told them that she was convinced Henneger took her sister and niece from his property, and may have either dumped them in the Connecticut River or—more likely—found a place to hide their bodies at one of the many construction sites he'd been working at back then.

Nicks thought it highly unlikely that Henneger would take the chance of bringing a boat out onto the water with the bodies of Suzanne and Becky Kerch on board, even if it were late at night. Further, even if he'd managed to dump their bodies into the river unseen—and they'd need to have been weighted down for that, too—the chance that they'd somehow come to the surface later on was something he thought Henneger would never risk. Evidence of this was the fact that he'd stayed in the area to this very day, apparently unconcerned.

That, for Nicks, was the key to the whole scenario involving Henneger: He must have been absolutely certain that no one would ever find the women's bodies for him to feel comfortable enough to stay put where he was, even if it was in an adjacent town. The bodies, Nicks was convinced, certainly weren't hidden on his former property in Hadley. The state police had done a thorough search of the place, including using GPR—ground penetrating radar—to scour the land around his house. Nothing came up.

All of this brought Nicks back to Sandy Whiting's other idea of the bodies having been hidden at a construction site. It was a desperate idea, he knew. The Hadley Police Department had overseen the search of the town's own dump, and they had also done a few cursory searches of other properties where illegal dumping took place. But they hadn't searched many of the sites where Pioneer Valley Contractors—Henneger's then-place of employ—had done work. Henneger might have had access to these sites after-hours, even if they'd been fenced off and padlocked.

That, then, is what Nicks decided to do. He'd start by paying a visit to Pioneer Valley Contractors and going through their records, searching for jobs they'd done at the time of Kerchs' disappearance. Then he'd arrange things from there.

As he strolled around a street corner, making his way back onto Main Street, he glanced around to catch his bearings. Continuing toward the rising sun would bring him back to King Street. He drew out his smartphone and checked the time. It was 7:28.

He started off again, heading back to the hotel.

****

Fielding settled in for breakfast at the Hotel Northampton's Coolidge Park Cafe. He'd found a pleasant place to sit on the outdoor patio there, and was reading through the files that Weirdlee had given him and Nicks the night before. His mind, though, was half on his work and half on his concerns regarding his new partner.

Nicks, he thought, was overly harsh with the sergeant at the Hadley police station. Banning was just doing his job ten years ago, and in all likelihood had been following protocols that were in place for just such a circumstance. You couldn't easily justify searching a property just because a woman missed a couple of days of work, and they *did* check up on things that Wednesday, as well as search Henneger's property that weekend.

So what was Nicks' beef?

He recalled having gone through his partner's service record before joining up with him in New York City. Nicks had been with the Bureau for five years prior, always with the Criminal Investigative Division (CID), and in that time he'd successfully investigated fourteen homicide cases, in addition to being involved in a handful of other criminal investigations. Fielding thought about that again as he sat there at breakfast. *The man was 14-and-O in murder investigations since joining the Bureau.*

He began to wonder about those cases, then. He recalled how Nicks had answered him with a definitive "Yes" when he'd asked him if he'd ever solved a cold case like this one before. Maybe Nicks had had a bad time in one of those. Maybe, Fielding mused, a similar circumstance had stirred up ill feelings inside of him, either during his time with the Bureau or sometime before he came on. It was something to consider, anyway, which was better than the alternative: that maybe the man was just cold-hearted jerk.

Still immersed in thought, Fielding didn't see Nicks

coming out from the Cafe's interior dining area. Nicks, coffee and lemon pastry in hand, strode up to Fielding's table and took a seat next to him.

"Morning, partner," he said to him.

Fielding looked up, surprised. "Hey there. Morning to ya."

Nicks took note of the opened file folder in front of Fielding, next to the agent's coffee and emptied breakfast plate. "Still reading up on things, huh?" he asked him, setting his coffee on the table.

"I suppose you stayed up all night doin' the same?" Fielding replied.

"Yeah. One of my habits."

Fielding smiled easily at that. He glanced about the patio, and then off to the nearby street, which lay quiet on that Sunday morning.

"So, what's on the agenda for today?" he asked. "Not much open by way of offices."

"No," Nicks agreed. "I'm going to go over Hadley to check out a few sites—the dump and some other places. I'd like you to find out a little more about this friend of Henneger's, the woman who rented his place while he was a guest of the state."

"You think she was more than just a renter?"

"Maybe. Maybe not."

Nicks looked off toward the center of town, visible just down the road from where they sat.

"Nice little town they got here. You should go for a walk yourself today."

Fielding glanced around. "Yeah. Maybe later." He looked back at Nicks. "You seen our Miss Weirdlee this morning?"

Nicks shook his head. "Nope. She'll be in touch, though, I suppose."

"You mean you ain't got no assignment for her today?"

Fielding asked, half teasing.

Nicks grinned back at him. "I'm not the boss of her. She was doing fine before we got here."

"Hell," Fielding shot back, "you're not the boss of me, either, come to think of it." He watched then as Nicks stared at him, straight-faced. "But you are the senior agent here," he said cheerily. "So I defer to your experience."

"Thanks for that, partner," Nicks replied.

****

Later on, after breakfast, Nicks drove first to the Hadley solid waste dump, a smaller-sized transfer facility located on North Branch Road along the southeastern bank of the meandering Connecticut River. Upon seeing the place, though, the agent immediately discounted the idea of Henneger having possibly used the location for nefarious purposes. With only one gate to get in there, and also being in a relatively exposed, open area, there was no way the man would take such a blatant risk. Nicks' visit there was brief.

There were other possible dumping grounds, and Nicks used some of the information Sandy Whiting had provided him to help navigate to the many different places in the area. Few appeared to be valid prospects, however—at least not for any long-term disposal of bodies. Henneger could have dumped them somewhere temporarily, Nicks supposed, until the intensity of the investigation subsided. But then he'd just be opening himself up to another risk of getting caught when going to retrieve and move them. Then again, Nicks considered that he, the meticulous investigator, might be thinking *too* methodically. If this truly was an unplanned crime, with the suspect desperately thinking of a way to get rid of the evidence, then he *could* have made a mistake after all, and then just got lucky in not getting caught at it.

The possibility also entered the agent's mind that Henneger could have destroyed the bodies outright by either burning them or, more grossly, sending them through a wood chipper or similar type of obliterating machine. One of the better-known urban legends, as well, involved killers dumping bodies into junked cars just prior to their being crushed. Again, though, that would probably take some planning—and probably after the crime took place—in order to carry it out. And since Henneger surely wouldn't attempt to burn the bodies on his property, would he alternatively risk carting them around while searching for a place to destroy them?

Nicks drove into South Amherst and found Station Road, taking that route for a ways before arriving at his destination. He pulled his car over at a dirt pullover, just before a small bridge where the little Hop Brook ran under. Sandy Whiting had told him that this was one of the places she suspected Henneger might have discarded the bodies of her sister and niece. He'd worked on a nearby bike path parking area—located just up the road from where Nicks had parked—as it was being built, and would be familiar with the area. Nicks left his car to go take a look around.

Pieces of trash lay strewn about here and there, he saw— most likely from passersby as they sped by in their cars. He walked along the road until he came upon the small bridge that spanned the brook. There, he looked off southward to the little stream that snaked into the wilderness, where tall weeds and marshy ground, thick with vegetation, surrounded the water on either bank. Walking farther along the road then, he took note of a horse farm set off on the left side. It appeared to be a riding lesson place of some kind, with no residence on the premises that he could see. Continuing ahead from there and returning his attention to the right side of the road, he came to a part of the treeline that appeared sparse enough for him to enter into the woods. He ventured into the trees.

The ground inside was layered with a thick blanket of ferns, and a variety of small treelets sprouted up here and there from the hidden earth. Advancing deeper into the interior, Nicks picked his way through a bramble of small bushes as he sought to get closer to the Hop Brook's meandering north bank. Upon reaching the top of the bank then, he stopped and looked down at the flowing brook, his gaze following its path as it fed through the swampy terrain.

The environment there conjured up memories for him. These types of wet forests—boggy and filled with creatures creeping and slithering about—were common in the eastern states. It was a place such as this, down in New Jersey, he recalled, where authorities had found a family—two boys and a father—half-buried in the muck. The father had killed his sons, they said, shooting them with a pistol at close range, before putting a bullet in his own brain to finish off the evil deed. In the months that passed after the crime, the bog began to claim their remains, sinking them deeper into the earth. Local police found the three during a search of the area later that winter. The place, they'd learned, was a favorite hunting area for the father. He'd suffered from depression, his wife told authorities, and had often fought with her and taken it out on the boys. When she finally told him just prior to the tragedy that she wanted a divorce and would push for full custody of the children, it was apparently too much for him to bear.

An open-and-shut case, it seemed, and that was the end of it for some years thereafter.

Then, four years later, an old friend of the family sent a

scathing letter to the state police, furious that they'd let the matter go. She'd also sent off a letter to the FBI, detailing how the mother had partied it up for months after the deaths, and adding that she had remarried just a year later. She also disputed the wife's claims about the father abusing his sons.

The Bureau assigned Nicks and his then-partner, Special Agent Barnes, to look into the matter. After interviews with various friends and family members, a clearer picture of the family's home life began to emerge. The wife had been unhappy with the marriage for months, and oftentimes neglected her two boys as she went out with friends after work and even on weekends. The father picked up the slack in spending time with the boys, but grew distraught over his wife's behavior. He sought out counseling, and he urged her to do the same in order to preserve the family. She refused, telling him instead that she wanted a divorce.

Something must have changed in her head, though, Nicks surmised. Perhaps it was the idea of paying child support if she gave up custody of the boys. Later analysis of the father's killing, then, showed that the angle of the shot fired at his head was too far forward for him to have naturally pointed the weapon at himself and pulled the trigger.

After another, more detailed round of questioning, the wife finally began contradicting herself just before lawyering up. Other people came forward, though. Some testified that she'd often lamented being married and having kids. She wanted to be free of it all.

And then Nicks uncovered the fatal flaw in her terrible scheme: After obtaining a search warrant for her smartphone, he found an exercise app on the device that tracked her activity each day. The phone itself was new, but she'd apparently had the same app installed on a previous phone, and, upon further investigation, he found the website where her personal data had been uploaded to and which also stored over five years of GPS tracking data. That data placed the woman at the scene of the crime on the same day the incident occurred. Under pressure then, she confessed to having committed the grisly murders.

Nicks looked all around him—to the trees and the thick weeds covering the moist ground. He listened to the little brook trickling along its way, and to the sounds of birds chirping in the quiet air.

There was nothing for him to discover out there on his own, he decided. He turned and walked back to the car.

****

John Henneger parked his beat up, faded blue 2000 Ford E-150 van on the curb outside of O'Brien's Pub and then walked into the little tavern to start his usual Sunday afternoon drunk. As he strolled inside, the same woman bartender who'd worked there on Saturday called out to him from behind the bar.

"Hey Johnny. You just missed that foxy girl."

"Huh?" Henneger said, glancing about.

The bartender pointed off to the street. "That FBI girl who asked about you yesterday? She just walked outta here. Took a left down the street."

Henneger quickly spun about and raced through the doorway to get back outside. Once on the sidewalk, he looked anxiously down the street, searching.

There, just a few dozen yards away, he spotted a woman with long, dark red hair just crossing the street. He sprinted ahead to catch up with her, but as the traffic between them picked up because of a nearby green light, he had to hold up before finding an opening to squirt across the street himself. He spotted her rounding a corner to get onto the little Manhan Rail Trail, which bisected the city's southern downtown area along Hampton Avenue. He ran ahead to get there.

Coming up to trail, he looked down its path. Trees and brush crowded the paved trail along either side. The way gradually led uphill and then bent to the right a bit near the top of its rise. He didn't see the woman walking there, so he figured she must have just rounded the corner. He raced on.

At the top of the rise, he could see down a good length of the path. Still, though, there was no sign of the woman. He slowed his pace then to a brisk walk, his eyes darting to the left and right just in case she'd left the trail. Following along the path for a ways, he looked down the embankment to his right, his eyes searching an apartment complex's parking lot there. He looked off to his left then and scanned the area around some townhouses on that side.

Nothing.

Hustling along, he passed by a young couple walking in the opposite direction. Shortly thereafter then, he came upon a park bench to his right. There, he looked down an embankment at a small city parking lot located at the bottom. His eyes scanned the cars parked there before he looked off across the street from the lot, over at the Paradise Brewery. There, he spied the woman standing just outside the brewery's entrance.

How the hell'd she get so far ahead of me?

She stepped inside the place.

Henneger bolted ahead, down the embankment, and ran across the parking lot to get to the brewery.

The interior of the Paradise Brewery had a clean, rustic feel to it, with a small, rectangular bar facing the left side and a collection of tables surrounding three sides of the bar. The kitchen was open-faced and directly behind the bar. Presently, a good number of people took up both the bar area and the tables.

Henneger rushed through the doorway, his eyes darting about, searching.

The bartender—a tall, overweight man dressed in the brewery's staff attire of black slacks and a brown golf shirt—noticed him looking for someone and called out to him.

"Can I help you?"

Henneger answered, "You see a redhead come in here?"

The bartender glanced around. "No. I didn't see anyone."

Patrons overhearing the exchange looked about. Some hunched their shoulders.

"She just came in. Just now," Henneger said.

The bartender put up his hands. "Sorry. I was working. I didn't see her."

"You sure she came in here?" asked a patron sitting at the bar.

"I saw her walk in the door, here," Henneger replied, pointed back at the entrance.

"Maybe she just walked through here," said another patron. He pointed off to a glass-paneled doorway at the back of the place. "She coulda gone that way."

Henneger walked briskly to the glass-paneled door. He grabbed onto its latch, pulled it down, then swung the door open and strode through it. Outside, he came upon the side of a multi-story, open-bay municipal parking garage directly in front of him. A wide pedestrian walk-through intersected the parking garage and brewery, and he first looked off to his right, only to see nothing that way. Then he looked to his left. There, he caught sight the woman at the end of the walkway, just rounding the corner of the rear of the parking garage to get onto a city street, beyond.

He ran ahead.

The open bays of the parking garage were such that it essentially had no walls to speak of, and so Henneger expected to be able to see the woman continuing along its back side, up the street's sidewalk. Look as he did for her, though, he couldn't see her there.

Coming around the corner to arrive on the street's sidewalk then, he looked up the road as it followed uphill on its way to meet up with the city's Main Street.

Nothing.

"Fuck..." he swore. How the hell could he have lost her with him being so close on her tail as he was? He looked upward at the garage, where a flight of stairs, also open, led up to the different levels of the garage. Still, though, he saw no sign of her.

He started up the sidewalk.

Following along the backside of the parking garage, Henneger stopped at its far corner and peered down a side alley there. This alley, like the other he'd just come from, was open all along its path. Again, though, he saw no sign of the woman. He continued up the sidewalk in a huff. The uphill incline steepened as he passed by a few small storefronts that lined the sidewalk on that side of the street. As he marched ahead, he peered through the glass doors and display windows of each store, checking. Then, almost at the top of the street, he spun himself around, frustrated. He glanced about the street, and then at the opposite sidewalk. Cars waiting in traffic lined the street itself, and people crowded the sidewalks on either side. Still, there was not a trace of the redheaded FBI girl. He turned and looked off across the intersecting Main Street then, scanning the storefronts on the opposite side of that street. The Blue Squirrel, Sam's Jewelry, the Wheatley Cafe, Skinny's

Tatts...nothing. She had disappeared on him again.

"Fuck!" he swore to himself once more. "What the hell?"

A wave of anger swept through his mind. He simmered there in silence for a moment as passersby walked past him in either direction. Then, resigned at having lost her, he headed back to O'Brien's to find out what the woman had been up to this time.

****

"Miss Weirdlee," Fielding called out as he walked along the sidewalk on Main Street. He was on the right side of the street, just a ways down from the Wheatley Cafe—a narrow, two-storied eatery whose first floor was in the basement and second level street-side. Presently, Weirdlee stood just outside of the entrance of the cafe, her eyes focused on an intersecting side street just across the way. As Fielding approached her, she turned and nodded to him, appearing not at all surprised at seeing him there.

Fielding had used "Miss" because he didn't want to out Weirdlee as a federal agent in public. Once he stood before her, though, she greeted him with no such discretion.

"Agent Fielding. Good to see you."

He smiled at her. "I was just walking around, looking for a good place for lunch."

Weirdlee glanced behind her and gave a nod. "Here is as good as any."

Fielding peeked through the open doorway. The place inside was narrow, with booth seats taking up the left wall all the way down, and a line of small, round tables lining the right wall. At the far end of the room, he could just make out the serving counter. The place was well attended.

"Okay," he said. "You up for lunch, too?"

"Sure."

They both went inside.

Inside, the two agents ordered a light lunch of sandwiches and fresh lemonade. They took a seat at one of the booths on the left wall.

"I really didn't expect to run into you this afternoon," Fielding said as he started on his ham sandwich.

Weirdlee's choice was turkey. "I tend to catch people off guard," she said, finishing her "guard" with that Boston accent of hers which leaves out the "r"s.

Fielding chuckled at that. "I bet you do."

They ate in silence for a little while, until Fielding started again.

"Nicks had me look up that woman who rented our guy's house during his stay in the lock up."

Weirdlee nodded as she chewed her last bit of sandwich.

"Lisa Saunders is her name. She's a nurse over at a local hospital, here abouts."

"Have you talked with her?" Weirdlee asked.

"Naw. I figured I'd wait till Nicks gets back, then we can see how to handle it."

"Good," said Weirdlee. She fetched her lemonade and sipped some of it from a straw. "Mr. Henneger is starting to get a little frustrated."

Fielding wiped his mouth with a napkin. "He is?"

"Mmm," Weirdlee purred. "We may need to interview him sooner rather than later."

Fielding grinned at her. "You've made him uncomfortable, have you?"

"Yes." Weirdlee smiled. "I do tend to do that to people, too—when it calls for it, of course."

Fielding looked down at the table, then glanced off to the cafe's entrance. "I took the time to look a bit further into our colleague's history, too."

Weirdlee looked at him, puzzled. "Nicks?"

He returned his attention to her. "Yeah."

"Hmm. Now why would you want to something like that, Agent Fielding?"

Fielding didn't answer her question. "He's a man on a mission, from what I read."

"Is he, now?"

"You know," Fielding went on, "I thought he was a bit overboard on the Hadley cops when we saw 'em yesterday. Come to find out, he's got a thing about small town cops knowin' their business. Or *not* knowin' it."

"Does he, really?"

"He's had problems with the local boys before. Seems to think they're not trained well enough to handle certain cases."

Weirdlee gave him an overly curious expression. "You mean...like how to decide when to take a call seriously or not?"

Fielding grinned back at her. He had a feeling she was toying with him. "You already knew?"

She replied with a nod, "I did."

Clasping his hands together on the table, Fielding asked her, "And what do you think, Agent Weirdlee? You think he's got any cause for feeling that way?"

Weirdlee considered his question, choosing her words. "I...suppose there are some small town police forces ill equipped for such things—missing persons, homicides and the like. Then I'm sure there are others that are fine with them. I think it depends on the force—how many officers they have, their budgets and training and so on."

Fielding kept a thoughtful pose. "Yeah...I suppose that's right. I guess that's pretty accurate."

Weirdlee smiled back at him. She took a sip from her lemonade then and sat back in her chair, placing her hands on her lap. "So..." she asked him, "who else have you been looking into in your spare time today, Agent Fielding?"

Fielding gave her a quick innocent look at first, before caving in and admitting, "Well, I did a little back-checkin' on you, too, truth be told."

Weirdlee smiled. "I suspect you did. And what did you find out about me?"

Fielding sat back, himself, and his once relaxed expression grew troubled. "Surprisingly little, actually. And I gotta tell ya, that's kinda got me a little concerned, to be honest."

"Oh really? How so?"

"Well," Fielding started, adjusting himself in his seat, "I went as far back as you comin' outta Brandeis about a year ago,"—he smiled at her— "which I guess makes you the junior agent, here." His smile quickly left him. "But your record gets redacted after that. Which I'm sure you're well aware of."

"Redacted..." Weirdlee said airily, flashing her eyebrows. "Sounds intriguing."

"Yeah, right. Now why would your history be classified from the time before you went to school?"

"Mmm," Weirdlee purred. "Would it make you feel better, Agent Fielding, to know that I grew up in a wholesome American home, with a loving family and a cat named, uh, Fluffy or something? Maybe I was even the homecoming queen."

Fielding kept a straight, emotionless expression. "I'll tell ya what, Agent Weirdlee. I grew up in a small town, and I worked hard and went to school. I grew up always tryin' to do the right thing, as best I could. I got me this career here in the FBI, and every time I can do it, I go home to my wife—who I love very much—and I thank God for giving me everything I got. All I'd like to know in return is that I got partners by my side who I can trust, and who aren't a part of some shady goings-on that I gotta worry about when we're in some dark alley somewhere."

Weirdlee looked on, unemotional as Fielding continued.

"You know what I really think about you, Agent Weirdlee?"

"What's that?" she replied.

Fielding glanced around guardedly, and he said to her in a hushed voice, "I think that Boston accent of yours is as phony as your red hair. I think you worked for the Bureau even before you got outta college, and I think Assistant Director Ledds got you up here to watch over myself and Special Agent Nicks."

Weirdlee laughed loudly at that. "Watch over you? You've got to be kidding me."

Fielding nodded. "Yeah. That's right. So why don't you just tell me what's really going on here. Who are you, really?"

"I'm afraid can't tell you anything you don't already know, Agent Fielding."

"Why not?"

Weirdlee leaned forward in her seat and said to him seriously, "Because it's classified."

Fielding huffed, "Son of a..."

Weirdlee sat back again. She picked up her lemonade and sipped the last of it. She said to Fielding, "You have nothing at all to worry about with me, Daniel. I'm not here to spy on you or Agent Nicks or anyone else I work with. I'm here to help solve a double homicide. That is all."

"You mean a missing persons' case," Fielding corrected her, "till we find the bodies."

Weirdlee eyed him thoughtfully. She whispered, "Naturally."

****

Henneger returned to O'Brien's Pub and walked up to the bar. The bartender met him there.

"Track her down, tiger?" she asked him, ribbing him.

"Shit," Henneger swore, "the chick is a ghost."

"Hard to get, huh?"

Henneger ignored the comment. He asked her, "What'd she want, anyway?"

The bartender shrugged. "I dunno. She didn't order anything." Then she looked over at Fred Duncan, who sat at his usual spot at the left end of the bar. "She sat next to Fred, though, and talked to him for a little while."

Henneger leered at the barfly. The guy had a big mouth, he thought, and was a sucker for a pretty face.

He walked briskly over to him.

The bartender asked Henneger, "You want a beer?"

Henneger answered as he came up to Fred. "Yeah. Gimme a Bud." Then he gave Fred a swat on the shoulder. "Chick came by to see you again, huh, Freddy?"

The snarl on his face made it clear that he wasn't pleased.

Fred was already heavily buzzed—even though it was still in the early afternoon. He looked at Henneger with a fractured smile, half-knowing he was in trouble.

"I, uh, yeah," he said. "She said hi to me."

Henneger nodded eagerly. "Bet she said more than that, chief. What'd you guys talk about? You been talkin' about me again?"

Fred took a chug from his beer. "Nope," he said, swallowing his fill. "She didn't even mention you this time."

That caught Henneger off guard. "She didn't?"

Fred shook his head. "She just asked about me. Asked me how I was doin'."

The bartender came over with Henneger's beer and set

the bottle down in front of him. "Tab, John?"

Henneger said to her, "Yeah," before turning his attention back to Fred. "So, what's the fuck with that? Why she asking about you?"

"I dunno," Fred said. Then he smiled big at Henneger. "Maybe she likes me."

Henneger slowly shook his head, frowning at the drunkard. "No. That ain't it."

Actually, that *was* it.

Joanna Weirdlee had a particular way about her, and she could sense innocence—or innocence lost—in most of the souls she encountered. Fred wasn't actually a bad man. He wasn't even tainted, really.

Twenty-seven years before, the then-young Fred Duncan had gotten himself drunk while out partying with his girlfriend at the time, Sheila Kent, and some friends. They were in downtown Northampton, and Fred and Sheila were heading back to her car for the short drive home. The parking lot where she'd parked her car was at the bottom of long, steep hill that fell away from a south corner of Main Street, nearby City Hall. A narrow flight of concrete steps led down there. Fred was about half way down the steps when he got distracted while playing around with Sheila, and he tumbled all the way down the stairway. *Hard.* An ambulance showed up and took him to the hospital, but the prognosis wasn't good. Fred had suffered serious head injuries, including damage to his vision and his hearing, as well as psychological issues, and, as feared, he did not respond well the therapy he underwent for several months afterward.

Diagnosed to be permanently disabled, Fred first had to leave college, where he'd been attending UMass at Amherst, and, a few months later, lost Sheila, as well. The latter circumstance was due largely to his behavior owing to his injury. Fred suffered from fits, and had bouts of angry outbursts that alarmed Sheila. Worse, she'd been pregnant with his child since before his injury, and with the baby's birth upcoming, she feared for both the baby's safety and her own. So she left Northampton—and Freddy—and moved off to Greenfield to start things anew.

For years following, Fred never saw his ex-girlfriend, nor visited with his daughter, Kelly. Fred's own family—a brother and a sister—lived closer to Worcester, and so he rarely saw them, either. He was all alone through the years, with only his damaged mind and just one other comfort adding to his life: his bar friends.

Never working full-time, Fred got to drinking every day, to the point where all he ever did was go to the bars. This quickly consumed his spare time—it being the only thing he had to look forward to in life. They humored him there and took care of him, buying him beers, and—for a time, anyway—feeling sorry for him. Later, some of his "friends," knowing he had income streaming in, got to expecting him to buy them beers. And he did. Lots of them. It was a mutually satisfying arrangement that eventually grew into a lifestyle for Freddy. Days quickly fell into weeks, weeks fell into months, and months into years, until, at last, over twenty years had passed him by.

It was only then that his daughter, now a young woman, came to visit her long-absent father one day. The two made amends, and thereafter—though there was still some acrimony—they spoke to each other from time to time, and Fred would even take a bus trip up to Greenfield once or twice a month to visit with her. Most times, though, he didn't stay for very long; there was always his bar friends to get back to, after all.

Inside of Fred's mind, all the while, all he ever comprehended were distortions of the reality going on around him. His vision was shortsighted, and, with damaged hearing, the voices he heard tended to sound muffled and hollow. The fits of anger that had tormented him earlier in his life, meanwhile, largely subsided as his frustration with his condition eventually fell away with the passing of time.

These days, Fred accepted who and what he was, entirely and without remorse. He was a drunk in a bar, wanting only for people to like him.

After another sip of his beer, Fred offered Henneger some more details of Weirdlee's visit with him.

"She asked me if I hang out here every day. I said 'what else am I gonna do?' and told her I'm on disability."

Henneger took a swig of his beer as he listened and Fred went on.

"She asked me if I was ever married, or if I had a girlfriend, and I said no." He smiled, adding, "Unless *she* said 'yes', to me." And he laughed at that. Then he sat there looking at his beer, and his smile faded. He whispered, "She sure is pretty. I wish I met someone like that."

Henneger gave him another swat on the shoulder. "She's trolling you, man."

Fred snapped his eyes to him. "Watcha mean, trolling?"

"Trying to get on your good side, you dumb ass. Milk you for information."

Fred crimped his face, confused. "But I don't know nothin'."

Henneger chugged some more of his beer. He looked around the bar, and then again to Fred. "Maybe you don't, you fuckin' drunk ass. Just don't be talking about me when I'm not around. Piss me off."

Fred nodded sheepishly. "Okay."

Henneger gave him a leering smile—not the genuine

kind, at all, but rather the kind a person makes when he thinks very little of you.

"Fuckin' dumbo."

7

Re-Searches

"Oh, God," Suzanne sighed, "I think he's selling pot again."

"Or worse," Sandy replied.

The two sisters sat at the kitchen table at Sandy's Connecticut home. It was the Saturday before the Fourth of July, 2004, and Suzanne had been visiting there for the day.

She sneered and shook her head at Sandy's suggestion. "He wouldn't get back into coke--no fucking way."

"Why not?" Sandy asked. "He could be selling heroin for all you know."

"*Nooo...*" Suzanne moaned. She took a swig of her Michelob Light. "I told him if he ever got back into that shit--or even coke--I'd leave him."

"Pot's bad enough, Suzy," Sandy argued. "You've got a kid in the house, for Christ's sake."

"He doesn't do anything in the house."

"What difference does *that* make? If he pisses people off and they start looking for him, that's where they'll go to find him."

Suzanne straightened herself in her seat. She knew that her sister was right about these things, but still struggled with her own stubborn denial.

"I'm not leaving him unless he proves it's not worth it to stick around. I can't afford a place of my own—not with Becky, too."

Sandy leaned forward in her chair, placing a hand on

her sister's. "You can stay here with us until you get resettled."

"*No*," Suzanne replied, pulling her hand away. "I'm too old for that shit. And I'm not pulling Becky out of school. She's just starting to make some good friends there."

Sandy smiled knowingly. "*Boy* friends?"

Suzanne flashed her eyebrows and allowed herself a grin. "Maybe," she said. Then she drank from her beer again before saying, "She doesn't like John, either, but it's not as easy as just pulling up our stakes and moving on. This is the first house I've ever had, Sandy. You want me to go back to living in some shitty apartment with people partying all fucking night long right next to me?"

"I want you to get away from John, Suzy. The guy's a loser. What do you think you're ever going to have with him?"

"A home and a yard," Suzanne replied tersely. "A place where Becky can bring friends over and not be embarrassed because everyone has to fit into a living room that doubles as a kitchen." She waved her hands around. "I never had any of this before, Sandy. And if I don't settle down, I'm never gonna have it. John isn't perfect—hell, he's not even what I hoped for. But he pays his bills and mows the lawn. He keeps me company most nights, and doesn't bitch when I go visit friends."

"That's only because he gets to go out, too."

"And what's so wrong with that? Look, sister of mine, we don't have the greatest relationship, but it's not the suckiest, either."

"No, not too bad," Sandy said in a mocking tone. "He just smacks you around when you deserve it, right?"

Suzanne pushed her beer bottle away and got up. "All right," she said in a huff. "I guess it's time for me to go."

Sandy realized she'd spoken out of line. "Oh, I'm sorry.

I'm sorry, Suzy. I shouldn't have said that."

Suzanne gathered up her purse. "Yeah, but you did. And I know what? Everybody else says that, too, and I know I'm an asshole for staying with him and whatever else the fuck I do."

As she strode over to the kitchen door, Sandy caught up to her and stopped her. "Suzy, please," she pleaded. "I'm sorry. I love you—you know that I do. I just don't want to see you getting hurt."

Suzanne let out a relenting sigh. It was always the same discussion, it seemed, no matter who she was talking to.

"Sandy," she said, "I gotta do what I gotta do. I love you, too. And I promise you, if he gets back into selling coke, then I'll leave him. If he sells *anything* out of the house, I'm gone. Okay?"

"I hope so," Sandy said, teary-eyed.

Suzanne smiled at her. "I'll see you in a few weeks. Paula's birthday, right?"

Sandy returned her smile. "My big first grader. She'll be leaving for college before I know it."

Suzanne laughed. "She sure will. And Becky will be doing that herself in a couple of years." She glanced off through the kitchen door's window then. "I do have to get going," she said. "Supper at the home front."

"Okay," Sandy said. "Drive safe and stay on the right."

Suzanne winked at her. "Right."

They hugged each other, and then Suzanne left Sandy's home to head back north to Massachusetts.

The two sisters would never see each other again.

****

Sam Nicks spent his Sunday afternoon driving about the towns of Hadley and Amherst. It was a peaceful, sometimes lonely trek along winding, picturesque country roads and small town streets, the latter oftentimes busy with people either enjoying the day off, going about errands, or just spending time with kids and family. At each stoplight, Nicks would glance at their faces as they gathered at crosswalks or huddled about each other for small town gossip. They all had their day-to-day lives to tend to, he knew—lives filled with appointments and shopping lists and schedules for the kids. They'd head out to the malls, or stop by the local Home Depot for a new screen door or another bag of lawn fertilizer. Some little girl or boy somewhere was having a birthday party in the backyard, just as Sandy Whiting's daughter had enjoyed the other day.

They all had their lives. They all had their hopes and their dreams, their heart-filled loves, and yearning aspirations. Teenagers were getting out of high school, and parents were becoming proud grandparents. Brothers argued over their favorite sports teams, and fathers desperately hoped their daughters didn't go out with that creep who'd stopped by the other day.

It was all so very ordinary, these things that went on in the world. And all so very wonderful, Nicks imagined, too.

And then, somewhere, someone was plotting a terrible crime. Someone wanted to end another person's life on this earth. These kinds of people were out there, the special agent knew, stalking the mothers and the fathers, and the trusting children who'd never known any better in their perfect little lives.

And how Nicks hated them so!

The destroyers of innocence. The predators, lurking in the darkest corners of this world, waiting to pounce on unsuspecting souls.

Nicks, for his own part, was but a simple man. Solitary in his motives. Was it justice, he wondered, that he searched for in hunting down these killers? Vengeance for the victims? Or was it merely some measure of self-centered satisfaction in knowing he'd at least done *something* good in his life?

The faces he'd seen in the past—sullen and miserable—all flashed across his mind. The tear-soaked eyes of families who'd been robbed of their loved ones—the anguish, the pain, and unendurable sorrow that he could never fully bring solace to. He saw Sandy Whiting's pale face, too, and he heard, again, her wails of anguish. And her husband, Richard, came up to them, holding his wife in his arms, and he asked the FBI agents for just one thing. One thing that Nicks knew they might never truly find.

And it wasn't justice, after all.

"We just want to have closure—*please*," Richard implored him that day, his voice choked with tears for the suffering of his wife.

That day had happened only yesterday as Nicks drove around on a warm and sunny Sunday afternoon. But it was every single day in his mind, too, as the voices and endless misery of dozens of other innocents stayed with him, always.

Driving him. Compelling him.

Begging him.

Nicks pulled into a self-storage lot off Route 47 in Hadley, just by the eastern banks of the Connecticut River. Ten years ago, Pioneer Valley Contractors oversaw the construction of the place. It was one of the sites Sandy Whiting had gone to the week her sister and niece went missing, when she'd desperately searched the piles of sand and gravel, the rows of Dumpsters filled with construction waste and garbage, and the ditches excavated for power lines and plumbing. At the time, the pouring of the slab for the facility, upon which the storage garages would be placed, hadn't yet started. And Sandy dug into the dirt with her bare hands, crying for her loved ones so cruelly taken away from her.

Nicks got out of his car and approached the fence of the storage place, named Midway Self Storage. The gate was closed and locked, for entry by renters only. He looked inside at the rows of garages, still appearing quite new even after nearly ten years of use. His gaze pierced the concrete slabs they rested on.

They have to be somewhere, he imagined of the victims.

Sometimes, you had to jar somebody to get him moving again. Henneger had seemingly gotten away with murder, and in all the years that had passed by since then, he'd had no reason to believe otherwise.

A seed of doubt would have to be planted in his mind, then.

And Nicks intended to give him one.

****

Monday morning began with Special Agent Nicks making a few phone calls, then heading out to the business office of Pioneer Valley Contractors. There, he requested information on all of the sites they'd worked on from the fall of 2003 to the fall of 2004. The company readily obliged, even providing the agent with schematics and blueprints of the sites. Armed with those, Nicks then contacted Guardian GPR, a company providing ground penetrating radar services in New England, and requested a team for a few select jobs he had planned. Special Agent Fielding, meanwhile, was busy at the county courthouse getting all of the prerequisite search warrants for the various sites.

It was after 10:00 AM when Hadley Police Chief Towers arrived at Midway Self Storage, the site of Nicks' first planned search. Fielding had not yet arrived with the warrants, but the owner of the facility, despite being irritated by the disruption, had allowed the GPR work to start without one.

Towers got out of his cruiser and approached Nicks, who stood off from the garage area just inside the property fence while watching the Guardian team go to work. The FBI agent was dressed a bit more casually on this warm morning, still with black slacks and a white dress shirt, but minus his jacket and tie, and with the shirt's long sleeves rolled up to his elbows. He kept his Glock 22 sidearm holstered on the right side of his belt. Dark sunglasses hid his eyes.

Towers appeared more than a little annoyed as he came up to him and asked, "Just what the hell are you doing here?"

Nicks wasn't bothered by the question. "Morning, Chief," he said. He looked off to the GPR team. "Just doing a search."

Towers glanced at the team himself. "My desk sergeant told me you called in with a list of sites you want to search?"

"Yeah, that's right."

The chief gave Nicks a curious look. "And just what do you hope to find here, Agent uh...?" he paused, forgetting Nicks' name.

"Nicks," the agent reminded him. "It'd be awful helpful to find human remains, actually. But I don't have any expectations."

"My sergeant said you called the Amherst PD, too, about some sites out there?"

"Yes, I did. And the Northampton police, as well."

Towers looked back at the GPR team, then again to

Nicks, disbelief etched on his face. "You know, the state police searched all these areas ten years ago, Agent, uh, Nicks."

"Yes, I'm aware of that. I'm just covering all the bases here."

The chief put his hands on his hips. "Well, I'm afraid I don't have much manpower to help out, so this could take a few of days."

Nicks gave nod and a wave of his hand. "Perfectly fine, Chief. I'll only need your guys for searches in the woods. These guys, here," he said, pointing at the GPR team, "can handle the open areas. At least until we come across something. Then we'll need to call in a dig team, of course."

Towers looked over at the paved storage pad. "Shit, they could get a reading on anything under there—pipes, wiring, or God knows what."

"That's true."

The chief shook his head. "Lot's of money. And this ain't no insurance claim. The FBI will be flipping the bill for this one."

Just then, Fielding pulled up in the agents' rented Chevy Impala. He got out and made straight for Nicks and Towers, search warrants clutched in his hand.

"All set," he said as he came up to the two men.

"Let the chief, here, have the warrant for this place, along with the other two places in town," said Nicks.

Fielding sifted through the warrants.

"What exactly do you think will come of all this?" Towers asked Nicks. "If we couldn't find a trace of those girls back when they were just gone missing, what makes you think you'll stumble across 'em now?"

Nicks eyed the chief plainly. "I don't think we will, really. I mean, there's always the possibility that something got missed all those years ago. But realistically, I'd agree it's a long shot."

Fielding handed Towers the warrants for the storage facility and the other two properties in town—a condominium complex and a nature trail.

"So what's all this for?" Towers asked, eyeing the warrants.

"Well," Nicks replied, "let's just say I want to make a little noise, and we'll see what kind of reaction we get from it."

Towers nodded slowly, getting it. "You think our guy will get nervous and check on things?"

"Maybe," Nicks said. "Worth a shot. And who knows? Maybe we'll come up something after all."

The sound of a speeding car screeching to a halt by the street curb alerted the men. Out of the vehicle then leaped Sandy Whiting. She raced towards the lawmen.

Towers looked at her, exasperated, before turning to Nicks.

"Dammit," he said to him, "did you tell the sister what you're doing out here?"

Nicks gave a nod. "I just told her we're doing some searches. Better hearing it from me than hearing about it on the news later on."

The chief clenched his teeth. "But we're not going to find anything—you said that yourself. And that woman, there, raised all hell ten years ago. God knows what she'll do now."

Whiting came up to the men. She ignored the chief entirely and looked directly at Nicks. "You guys find anything yet?"

Nicks shook his head. "No, Mrs. Whiting. We've only just got started."

Whiting pulled a piece of folded paper from her front jeans pocket and unfolded it. She shook it in her hand. "Are you searching all these places I told you about?"

Nicks nodded. "Yes, ma'am. We've got all that taken care of."

"Mrs. Whiting," Towers said, "this could take a few days. You didn't have to drive all the way up here."

Whiting scowled at him. "I'll be here for as long as it takes—*officer*."

"Chief Towers," the chief reminded her. "And like I said, it could be a few days."

"He's right, Mrs. Whiting," said Nicks. "I didn't mean for you to drive all the way up here today. We'll probably only be searching a couple of sites per day."

"Then I'll just get a motel room," Whiting said defiantly. "But I'm staying here." She glanced at Towers. "I'm not going to let 'em screw it up for a second time."

Towers rolled his eyes.

Whiting pulled out her iPhone from her rear pocket. "Better call my husband and let him know my plans. Looks like I'll be taking some vacation days, too."

She stepped away then to contact her husband.

Towers turned to Nicks. "The press will probably be here pretty soon. News spreads fast. I better get an officer over here." He turned away to use his chest-clipped radio mic.

Nicks looked at Fielding, who'd remained quiet during the latest exchange. "You got that info on that woman who rented Henneger's house?"

"Yeah. Name's Lisa something-or-other. She lives in a town on the other side of Northampton."

"Give the address to Agent Weirdlee so she can pay her a visit. I'd like to know when exactly she moved into Henneger's place, and why she did, too."

"*Why?*"

"Yeah. I'm assuming she needed a place to live and wasn't just doing him a favor. Or...maybe she was."

Fielding nodded. "All right. I'll get in touch with her.

What do you want me to do with these?" he asked, holding up the remaining warrants.

"Drive out to Amherst and give 'em to the cops there. They said they'd need to call in the state police to help out with their searches. That's fine."

"Right. You staying out here, then?"

"Yeah," Nicks said. "I'll stick with these guys." He gave a nod to the GPR team.

Fielding started back to their rental car. "All right. See you in a bit."

Nicks turned to watch the GPR team at work. His attention, though, was quickly diverted to Sandy Whiting, off to his right, who was still on the phone and in a rather animated conversation. Apparently, her husband wasn't taking the news of her plans very well.

Nicks eyed her thoughtfully. She was a far different woman on this day than the one who'd broken down that past Saturday. She seemed determined—angry, even. He hoped, then, that he hadn't created a false sense in her head that the FBI was going to make everything turn out okay for her and her family. Nicks knew that finding the remains of her loved ones was still a huge long shot. Searching the same sites that had been searched ten years prior wasn't likely to yield any different results than before, just as the chief had said. His one hope was that all of their digging around again would prompt Henneger to recheck things on his own—maybe second guessing where he'd actually hidden the women's bodies. And, although Mrs. Whiting's presence there might complicate things, he understood the anguish, frustration, and anger that burned inside of her. She wasn't looking for closure, as her husband had asked for. She wanted justice.

And Nicks was going to do everything in his power to make sure she got it.

****

Assistant Director Ledds sat comfortably behind his desk in his office at the J. Edgar Hoover Building in Washington DC. A hot cup of coffee was set on the desk to his right as he looked over a report on his desktop computer. The start to another work week was well under way.

His phone rang. He reached over and picked it up.

"Assistant Director Ledds."

The voice of his secretary came through on the other side.

"Assistant Director, the Boston field office S-A-C is on the line."

Ledds sighed. He sat up in his seat and pushed his computer keyboard farther onto his desk to rest his elbows there. "Put him through."

"Yes, sir."

The line clicked, and Special Agent Solomon Ghents, in charge of the FBI's Boston field office, came on.

"Marvin, good morning to you, sir."

"Morning, Solomon. What can I do for you today?"

"Well, sir, it's come to my attention that you've brought up a team from New York City to look into a case out here in western Massachusetts."

Ledds nodded. "Yes, that's right."

"I, uh, was wondering why a team from my office wasn't assigned for that one. That's my jurisdiction."

"So it is, Agent Ghents. I'll tell you, I was passing through there a couple weeks ago while on vacation, and I kinda fell upon this old case out there. I thought it would be perfect for this guy I put on it. He's an up-and-comer in my Criminal Investigations Division. A real hot shot. I also got a girl from my office out there. It's her first time in the field, but I think she's really something special."

"Yeah..." Ghents mulled, "I just got a call from the local PD out there, town of Hadley. The chief there's a little bothered by your man. Says he's got all these searches going on out there."

Ledds shrugged. "So?"

"Well," Ghents began, chuckling uneasily, "he said something about putting the expense on our tab, here. We're not even involved in the investigation. It was the first I'd heard of it, in fact."

"Oh, well, sorry about that, Sol. The paperwork is in the funnel. Look, if things go well with this guy, Nicks, and his partner, I'm thinking of starting something. I think them two and that girl I put out there with 'em can do some good things."

"I see. I guess I'd feel a little better if we had someone over there with them, is all."

"Actually, Sol, I'd rather you not. Not unless they ask for assistance. Nicks has a lot of experience in the field, and the woman I got with 'em, Special Agent Weirdlee, has got a lot of potential on her own. She's young and full of verve, if you know what I mean."

Ghents replied, not so enthusiastically, "Yeah..."

"Listen, Sol, I'll have Nicks keep you in the loop out there, and I'll let him know that if they need any help he can call on you guys. How's that?"

"Well," Ghents sighed, "I guess that'll have to do."

"Good," Ledds said with a smile. "I'll let you go, then. Have a great week."

"Yeah," said Ghents. "You too."

****

John Henneger was a man of few words, and he was not one to be messed around with, either. Most people who knew him understood that about him, and for those who didn't know it, they were quick to find out.

Monday afternoon was a short workday for Henneger and the other workers employed by Carter Concrete and Landscape. They'd been spreading cement on a front walk that lined the shops of a new strip mall along Route 9 in Hadley, and by 2:30 PM they were just finishing things up there. The only thing left to do then was to clean up the site.

As he washed his hands in a bucket of water, Henneger's site boss, Paul Lindley, walked up to him.

"John," he said seriously, "can I see you a sec?"

Henneger replied, "Yep," and stepped aside with Lindley.

"Listen, man," Lindley said, "Rocky called me and said the fuckin' FBI called the office asking about you."

"Shit," Henneger swore, shaking his head.

"What's *that* all about?" Lindley asked.

"Aw, they're just fuckin' with me, Paul. Probably sniffing around to see if I'm selling crack or somethin'."

Lindley's eyes bulged. "Are you?"

Henneger sneered at him. "No. Hell no. I ain't done shit since I got out. They're just out to get my ass."

"The *FBI?* Why would they care about a small timer like you?"

"Fuck you, man. I've knocked some heads in my day."

"Take it easy," said Lindley, putting up a hand. "It's just kind of weird that the FBI would be asking about you. I'd think the state police would—"

"Fuck them guys," Henneger interrupted. "They got nothin' on me. What the hell did they want, anyway?"

"Rocky said they wanted to know how long you worked here and what sites we were working on these days."

"And I suppose that old fatass told 'em everything they wanted to know."

Lindley lifted an eyebrow and gave a *no shit* expression. "They're the FBI, man."

Henneger wiped his hands on his jeans and started to walk away.

"Yeah, well," he said, "they're tryin' to set my ass up, I think."

He looked off to the worksite, then glanced back at Lindley. "We all set to quit today?"

"Yeah." Lindley nodded. "Just thought you'd want to know. Go out and have a few beers, man."

"Gonna do just that," Henneger called out as he made his way to his van. Hopping inside, he fired it up and put it in gear. He drove off the site in a cloud of dust, heading west back toward Northampton.

Driving along on his own, his mind began swirling with a simmering and growing rage. He considered himself a smart man—smarter than most, anyway, and certainly smarter than the cops who'd been harassing him. They were fishing, he was sure of it. Just trying to find something on him—anything—to put him back behind bars. This, for their screw up in not nailing him for whacking Suzy and Becky.

Oh yes, he'd killed those girls, sure enough. And damn near every day he still thought about it, one way or another. He'd given Suzy one hell of a beating that night before she finally went limp on him. It was incredible, really. One minute she was screaming away at him, and the next, suddenly quiet. He could still hear Becky yelling up the stairs for her mom, asking if she was okay. Then she screamed even louder at him, her soon-to-be killer, to leave her alone.

Leave her alone? What the hell was she thinking?

The foul names that little girl called him, swearing at

him like she did. Poor thing had no idea what was coming to her.

Henneger's mind shifted then to Freddy's comments.

'*Maybe she likes me,*' Fred had said to him, speaking of that hot-assed FBI girl everyone was talking about.

Fuck you, Freddy.

Still, the FBI was snooping around for something. At first he thought it was just another drug sweep—one of those nationwide things. But they wouldn't be asking people questions all over the place and letting everyone know they were around if that were the case. So they must have had something else up their ass that was making them move.

The FBI, for crying out loud.

Didn't they have anything better to do? And there was Fred, talking to that girl, too—probably yapping away every time she batted her eyelashes. What the fuck was he thinking? The backstabber.

Boy needs to shut his mouth.

Henneger drove past a few more storefronts. There was somebody else, too, he decided, who might need a little talking to.

He drove across the Calvin Coolidge Bridge, leaving Hadley behind. Driving through the center of Northampton then, he continued northwest along Route 9, making his way to the neighboring town of Florence. Turning onto a couple of side streets there, he pulled into the parking lot of a small apartment complex, then parked his van.

The units there were all small, single-story affairs, with stairs leading up to a raised apartment level. Each unit also had a small storage cellar, a window for which was set to the right of the stairs.

Henneger got out of his van and looked around. The

parking lot had just a few cars parked about the place. It was still late afternoon, too, so most people hadn't gotten home from work yet. He walked ahead then and up the stairs to Apartment 12. A window next to the door had its shades drawn closed. He pressed the doorbell button. A double-ding rang from inside.

No response.

He pressed the doorbell again. *Ding-ding.*

The window shades drew away, and a woman of about medium height with short blonde hair peeked outside. Still dressed in her nurse's uniform after having just got off work, her eyes went wide at the sight of Henneger, obviously not pleased to see him.

"What do *you* want?" she asked him through the window.

"Open up," he said with a bat of his hand. "Gotta talk to you."

She looked at him suspiciously for a moment. She hadn't seen him in months, so she figured something must be up. Reluctantly, she moved to the door and opened it for him.

Henneger eyed her with a scowl as she stood before him. He jabbed a finger at her. "You and I need to get things straight again, girl."

****

Midway Self Storage had turned up empty on the GPR search, and so Nicks had the team pack up their gear and head over to the second and final search site for the day. This was a condominium complex located off Mill Valley Road in Hadley, named Valley Heights Condominiums. Pioneer Valley Construction had contracted some work out there at about the same time of the Kerch girls' disappearances. The complex received new patios and storage sheds at sixteen of its units, and several sidewalks and walkways were also put in.

As at Midway—and likely, too, all the other places they'd go to—the chance of finding anything there was exceedingly slim. Then again, that wasn't the point of it all, anyway.

The press had made their first appearance earlier in the afternoon, with a television crew showing up at Midway Self Storage to break the news to the locals. By the time Nicks got things going over at the condominium complex then, nearly all of the local newspapers in the area had sent out reporters to the cover the unfolding story.

Fielding had rejoined his partner by this time, and he walked around on his own at times, curiously watching the GPR search team do their work. Sandy Whiting was there, too, of course. She'd found her station at a sidewalk bench and stayed there for the most part, only occasionally getting up to get a closer look at the GPR work. Earlier, while everyone broke for lunch, she'd made arrangements at the Clarion Hotel, just off the highway in Northampton, for the week.

It was a boring afternoon. Nicks referred the media to Hadley Police Chief Towers, making no comments himself. The area the search team worked in eventually filled up with curious onlookers, too—mostly residents of the condos—though, as it was a dull scene, most just took pictures and then wandered off.

Nicks eyed the shifting crowds every now and then, searching the faces. He suspected it was possible Henneger might stop by at one of these search locations, unlikely as that may be. Chances were, in fact, that on this first day of searching, he might not have even heard about them yet.

Still. People talk, and word gets around.

He took out his smartphone and checked the time. It was 3:15 PM. Special Agent Weirdlee, he knew, was also on the job and doing her own thing that day. Weirdlee was an unusual addition to his team, and he wondered what Assistant Director Ledds was really up to in assigning her there along with him and Fielding. Most of the background work she did could have been done in Washington, D.C., he figured, and the few interviews she'd conducted with the locals thus far could have just as easily been done by either himself or Fielding.

There was a presence about her, though, that intrigued Nicks. He was quite certain she was not at all what she appeared to be. There was no record, he'd learned, of her having participated in any other investigations prior to this one. Could that really be true, though? Or was her name simply redacted from any past cases?

She'd been a secret project for Ledds, it seemed, since joining the Bureau. The old man had kept her hidden away for some time—away from any who might ask questions of her or dig into her past. Until now, that is. For whatever reason, he was finally letting her out into the light.

The GPR team stopped.

The team leader called out to Nicks, "Got a candidate, here."

Nicks snapped out of his musing and hurried towards them.

8

Lisa Saunders

Thirty minutes had passed since Henneger went into the apartment of Lisa Saunders. He came out of the front door then, still talking to her as he held the door open. He nodded a couple of times to her, then he turned and walked down the flight of stairs to the front sidewalk. He made his way to his van. As he walked, he glanced about guardedly, watching for anything resembling the law. Just a couple of cars were there, he saw, parked in different areas of the lot. No cruisers. No beat walking cops. And no little yellow Ford Focus parked across the way, either. To his eyes, it simply wasn't there.

Special Agent Weirdlee sat in her car, her black-rimmed sunglasses hiding her eyes as she watched Henneger walk over to his vehicle and get inside. He started up the engine, backed out, and drove off.

Weirdlee looked over at Apartment 12. She took off her sunglasses and set them on the dashboard. Then she got out of the car and made for the apartment.

Lisa Saunders popped open a Michelob Light and was about to sit on her couch and watch some TV when the doorbell *ding-dinged*. She sighed, then walked over to the front window. Spreading open the shades, she saw Weirdlee standing there. The agent wore a black, pinstriped pantsuit with a white blouse underneath. Her maroon lipstick perfectly complemented her dark red hair.

"What do you want?" Saunders asked her through the

window.

Weirdlee reached into her jacket pocket and pulled out her ID billfold. She flipped it open and showed it to Saunders.

"Special Agent Weirdlee," she said to her. "FBI."

Saunders' face went pale. She swore to herself, *Shit*, before saying aloud, "Just a sec."

She opened the door and took in a big gulp of air before greeting the FBI agent.

"What can I do for you?"

"Lisa Saunders?" Weirdlee asked her.

"Yes, that's me."

"Can I come inside, Ms. Saunders?"

Saunders stared at her, still shaken up at the sight of the FBI badge. "Uh, yeah. Yeah, I guess so."

She stepped back to let the agent inside.

"Ms. Saunders," Weirdlee began as she walked into the apartment, "I'd just like to ask you a couple of questions. I won't take up much of your time."

Saunders nodded uneasily. "Okay," she said, closing the door. She set her beer down on a small table by the window.

Weirdlee looked at her, observing her demeanor.

"I noticed you just had a visitor here," she said to her, a flair of her Bostonian accent evident.

"Yes. Just a friend."

"That was John Henneger," Weirdlee confirmed.

Saunders swallowed, and she replied hesitantly, "Uh...yes, it was John." She reached for her bottle of beer and picked it up to drink from it. "He just stopped by to say hi."

"I see," Weirdlee noted. "Just a 'hello,' was it?"

Saunders nodded. "Yeah. That's all."

"Actually," Weirdlee continued, "as coincidence would have it, I'm here to talk about John." She looked casually about the small living room. "We're trying to clear up some details from a few years back, and we were hoping you could help us out."

Saunders chugged on her beer before responding. "I don't know if I can help you very much. We're not that close, really. I just know him as a friend."

Weirdlee turned to Saunders. "And as a renter, too."

Saunders stared back at her. "Yeah, a few years back."

Weirdlee smiled. "And how exactly did you come to rent from Mr. Henneger, anyway? I assume you two were friends before then?"

"Yeah, we were friends. We both knew the same people at a bar we used to go to. I had a studio apartment back then, and it was hard to pay for. John offered me his place—real cheap."

"Because he wouldn't be using it himself for a few years," Weirdlee finished.

Saunders looked down at her beer. "Yeah."

Weirdlee pulled out a small notepad and pen from her left jacket pocket to start taking notes. "And your apartment was in Northampton, yes?" she asked, already knowing the answer.

"Yes, that's right. Downtown."

"And how long did you live there?"

Saunders thought about it. "Uhh, maybe four months. Not long. I lived with my aunt and uncle before that, while I was going to college."

"In Northampton, too, or...?"

"Yes. They let me stay there for a little while, 'cause they go back and forth to Florida. But I wanted a place of my own, so I got the studio apartment in the summer. I didn't realize how hard it would be to get by on my own, though, so when John offered me his place cheap, I said 'sure'."

"And when exactly did you move into Mr. Henneger's

home?"

At that, Saunders shrugged her shoulders. "I dunno. It was in the late fall. He was sent away that November or December, I think?"

"Fall of 2004?" Weirdlee asked, writing on her pad.

"I think so. Was it 2004? Whatever year he got sent to jail."

"And you didn't move into the house prior to his arrest and incarceration, correct?"

"No, I didn't. They kept him in the local jail, here, till he got sent away."

"What about when he got out of prison, Ms. Saunders? Did you stay on for a little while, then?"

"Uh...for about a month, if that. Until I could find another place."

"Was he kicking you out?"

Saunders shook her head. "No, not at all. I just wanted a place of my own."

"I see. And you found this place here?"

Saunders watched Weirdlee's note-taking. "Actually, I roomed with a friend for a couple of months before I found this place."

Weirdlee gave her a curious look. "You moved out of Mr. Henneger's house to stay with someone else?"

Saunders nodded quickly. "A friend of mine—a girl. It's better having a woman roommate, you know? At least until I found my own place."

"Sure," Weirdlee agreed. "Were you and Mr. Henneger friends for very long before he offered his place to you?"

"A few years—maybe five or six. But we were more like bar friends, you know?"

"Mhhm. And you never dated him?"

"No. We never dated or anything like that."

Weirdlee closed her notepad, then stuffed both it and

her pen back into her jacket pocket.

"Were you with him on the same weekend his girlfriend, Suzanne Kerch, and her daughter disappeared?" she asked. "I mean, maybe drinking with him at a bar, or...wherever?"

Saunders shook her head. "I don't remember. That was a long time ago. I feel real bad about what happened, though. Is that what this is all about?"

Weirdlee raised an eyebrow. "Why do you feel real bad, Ms. Saunders?"

Saunders looked back at her, taken aback by the question. "I don't know. They disappeared, right? That's sad."

"Yes, it is. If something bad happened to them. You don't happen to recall seeing Suzanne that weekend, do you?"

"No. And honestly, I really didn't know her that well. I hadn't seen her in weeks before everything...well, you know."

"Yes, okay."

Weirdlee sighed, her eyes darting around the place once more. "Well, I guess that's it for now, Ms. Saunders. We'll be in touch if there's anything more we need." She turned and stepped over to the door, opening it.

"Sorry I couldn't have been more help," Saunders said.

Weirdlee paused at the door and turned to Saunders. She gave the woman's uniform a once-over look.

"Been a nurse for long?" she asked her.

Saunders glanced down at her uniform and replied, "Oh, about four years."

Weirdlee smiled. "I once thought about becoming a nurse. Knowing you're helping so many people—keeping them healthy and alive, so they can be with their friends and family who love them so very much. It must make you feel really good inside, knowing you're a part of that."

Saunders eyed the agent uneasily. She replied, "Yes. It does."

Weirdlee sighed once more, then glanced outside. "I only hope we can find Suzanne and Rebecca," she said airily. "Reunite them with their loved ones."

Saunders only stared back at her.

"Good day, Ms. Saunders," Weirdlee said.

Saunders waited for Weirdlee to step outside before walking ahead and closing the apartment door. She turned and pressed her back against it then and brought her hands up to her face, cupping them over her mouth and nose. She shuddered, and then, clasping her hands together, she looked up at the ceiling above her, and so on to the heavens beyond, where she knew Suzanne and Becky Kerch were surely looking down on her.

Tears trickled down her cheeks.

****

A false alarm. That's all it was.

The GPR team had picked up an aged cast iron sewer conduit that had been part of a line bringing wastewater from the buildings formerly on the site to the main line under the street. Referring to an old city schematic they'd obtained, the team was able to identify the object without having to dig.

Sandy Whiting, disappointed, retreated to her car, sitting there for a while before driving off at about 3:30 PM.

Nicks and Fielding, meanwhile, spent much of the rest of the afternoon in their rental car. Fielding passed the time browsing the Kerchs' old case files on his laptop. Nicks mostly just sat quietly in the driver's seat, his elbow propped up in the open window as he watched the GPR team. His mind, no doubt, was on other things.

"Once we get done with these searches, what else do ya got planned for the investigation?" Fielding asked his partner.

Nicks took a moment to ponder the question.

"Well..." he said at length, "these are just redos. I'd like to get some new searches in, too. There's some sites I have in mind—places Henneger goes to for vacation, things like that. We'll need to interview a few more people, though."

"Weirdlee talked to a few," Fielding reminded him.

"Yeah. She's still going around, too." Nicks checked his smartphone for the time, which presently read 4:05 PM. "She should have talked with that renter by now. I'll give her call in a few minutes and have her meet us back at the hotel for an update."

"Right," Fielding said. "When we gonna interview Henneger?"

"Maybe tomorrow. Weirdlee's got him itchy from all her snooping around, so we'll let him stew for a little while longer. We'll head over early tomorrow morning, maybe, before he goes to work, depending on what Weirdlee has for us."

Fielding nodded, then turned his attention back to his laptop. "All right."

Nicks looked back out the window at the GPR team, which appeared to be finishing up their search. Having them out there was a hefty expense for what was likely just a ruse. But, at the very least, all of the bases would be covered.

All of the bases.

Nicks wondered if that could ever be true. How many clues had been missed in the original investigation? How much evidence had been lost? The local police, he concluded, had been ill prepared for the case that fell into their laps all those years ago. As everyone in law enforcement knew, there was actually no such thing as a "waiting period" on missing persons investigations. That notion was just a myth borne on television shows and mystery novels. So this, Nicks determined, was all on the locals. It had been their decision to take Henneger's word for it—that the girls had gone off on their own. It was their decision not to search his property until that following weekend. And their decision to—

A text alert *beep* jarred Nicks from his thoughts. He pulled out his smartphone, there to see a new text message from Agent Weirdlee.

Talked to Lisa Saunders. See u back at hotel?

Nicks looked out the car window. The GPR team, he saw, was gathering up their gear. Their team leader would then report to him for any new instructions before calling it a day.

Turning back to his smartphone, Nicks replied to Weirdlee's text.

Yes. Be there in 30 minutes.

K, Weirdlee replied.

Nicks turned to Fielding, who was still engrossed in his case file studies. "Let's wrap this up," he said to him. "Them guys are about finished out there. We'll have 'em start on the Northampton landfill in the morning."

"Landfill?" Fielding replied, knowing that a dump was likely to be loaded with positive hits. "That oughta be fun."

Nicks grinned back at him. "A part of the job, partner."

****

Sandy Whiting walked into O'Brien's Pub, where the day-shift crowd had just begun filling in the seats. Right away, she saw John Henneger sitting at the bar, there amongst his drinking buddies. She strode up to him.

"Enjoy your beer, Henneger," she said contemptuously. "They don't serve it in prison."

He spun around to face her. "What?" he said, before recognizing who it was. "What the fuck are *you* doing here?"

She scowled at him. "I'm not afraid of you, you asshole."

He glared back at her. "Fuck you."

The bartender—the same one who had served Agent Weirdlee on her first visit there—hurried over to the scene.

"Hey, don't start here!" she yelled to Whiting.

Whiting ignored her.

"The FBI's on the case now, you fucker. They're gonna put you away."

"Oh, shut up," Henneger snapped back.

"Get out of here," the bartender demanded of Whiting.

Another patron sitting two stools away from Henneger leaned over to offer his own two cents to Whiting.

"Take off, bitch. Don't start your shit in here."

Whiting flipped him off with a "Fuck you," and again looked to Henneger. "You're going to hell, John. You fucking murderer."

Henneger abruptly stood up from his stool. Whiting stepped back.

"You gonna hit me, John?" she asked him. "You gonna put me down like you did my sister?"

"Get outta here!" the bartender yelled, pointing at the door. "Get the fuck out before I call the cops."

"Go ahead and call 'em!" Whiting yelled back. "What are they going to do? Protect a murderer—like they did before?"

"Go fuck yourself," Henneger snarled. "Kiss my ass and take a walk."

The bartender ran over to the bar's phone. "I'm calling the cops."

Whiting glared at Henneger, hatred radiating from her

face. "They're gonna put you away this time, you fucking asshole. The FBI is going to kick your ass."

Henneger jabbed a finger at her. "*You're* gonna get your ass kicked, you crazy bitch, if you don't get the fuck outta here."

"Oh, do me a favor and do it," Whiting said. "Give me a reason sue your ass."

The patron sitting next to Henneger grabbed his arm. "Fuck her, John. Let it go. The cops are on the way."

Just then, Fred Duncan walked into the place. He looked at Henneger and then to Whiting as they confronted each other. He stood off to the side of the door. "What's going on?" he asked.

"The cops are on their way," declared the bartender, hanging up the phone. She looked at Whiting. "You better get your ass outta here."

Whiting glanced around the bar, eyeing everyone staring at her—most of them contemptuously. "Fuck you all," she swore. "You're all a bunch of assholes."

She turned and stormed out of the bar.

The place remained quite for a few tense seconds.

"Jeezuz," said a patron near the jukebox, "what a fuckin' psycho bitch."

"Asshole..." the bartender swore.

Henneger settled back onto his bar stool. "Fuckin' whacko."

Fred walked up to the bar then, just next to Henneger. He ordered his usual beer. While the bartender fetched it for him, he turned to Henneger, looking at him sheepishly.

"Haven't seen *her* in a while, huh?"

Henneger glared at him. "Crazy little bitch. She thinks the Feds are gonna do something. They're just covering their own asses." He gave Fred a nod. "What about you, you asshole? You seen that fuckin' FBI chick again?"

Fred straightened himself. "Uh, nope. Not since the other day."

Henneger took a swig of his beer, then said to him, "Just keep your mouth shut. You don't know shit, so don't act like you do."

The bartender put Fred's beer down in front of him and he clutched onto it. He said to Henneger in a nervous stutter, "I know. I ain't said nothin' to her."

Henneger eyed him again. "Just be sure you don't, retard, or I'll give 'em a reason to arrest me after I take your ass out—and I mean for good."

****

That early evening, Nicks and Fielding found a table at the Wiggins Tavern. There, they waited for Weirdlee to arrive. Just after they ordered their drinks then, she showed up and Nicks waved her over to their table.

"Sorry I'm late," she said, taking a seat.

Nicks smiled back. "No problem. We just ordered drinks."

Fielding eyed Weirdlee admiringly as she opened up her menu and began perusing her choices. Dressed in her pinstriped pantsuit and with her dark red hair and matching red lipstick, she looked exceedingly attractive to him in the dim light of the tavern. He wondered then if she were married or dating someone. She wore no ring on her finger—which meant nothing to him, of course, considering her mysterious history.

"Your eyes are burning a hole through my menu, Danny Fielding," she said to him, still browsing options.

He sat up in his chair, flustered at having been caught in the act. "Yes, uh—sorry about that," he stammered. "You're lookin' lovely this evening, Agent Weirdlee."

She laughed at his formality. "Agent Weirdlee?" Then she lowered her menu and eyed both men. "Can't we get over all the formalities of the Bureau, boys, at least for after hours? Let's be friends, shall we?"

"Sounds good to me," Fielding said, smiling.

"As long as we don't *forget* we're in the Bureau," said Nicks, looking from Weirdlee to Fielding, and then eyeing the young male agent with a playfully suspicious glare.

Fielding caught his expression and protested, "I'm a happily married man, Agent—"

"Take it easy, *Danny*." Nicks laughed. "We're all friends here, remember?"

"Yeah," Fielding chuckled uncomfortably. "Sure we are."

The waitress came by and Weirdlee got in both her drink order, white wine, and her dinner choice. The men rattled off their own dinner choices, as well, and the waitress took those before leaving the table again.

"So..." Weirdlee began, "I had a talk with our Lisa Saunders this afternoon."

Nicks looked at her with interest. "Yes. How did that go?"

Weirdlee raised an eyebrow. "Guilty as sin, I think."

"What?" Fielding said, surprised.

"She gave you that feeling, did she?" asked Nicks.

"Oh, yes. Nervous as hell."

"That doesn't make her guilty of anything," Fielding said.

Weirdlee looked at him. "Our guy, Mr. Henneger, left her place just after I got there."

"Shit," Fielding swore.

"I noticed his van in the parking lot when I got there," Weirdlee said. "I waited for him to leave before going in to see Ms. Saunders."

"She's involved in some way," Nicks said, looking to

Fielding.

Fielding gave a nod. "I think you're right."

"She's breakable," Weirdlee offered.

"Think so?" Nicks asked.

"Oh, yes."

The senior agent tapped the table, considering things. "Let's follow through with the original plan, first," he said. He looked at Fielding again. "We'll have an early wake up tomorrow morning and go see Mr. Henneger for ourselves."

"Sounds good."

"What do you want me to do?" asked Weirdlee.

"*You?*" Nicks asked, feigning puzzlement. "Doesn't Homeland Security already have your itinerary planned out?"

She smirked at him. "Very funny."

He eased up on her. "Let's keep interviewing people around Henneger. How far have you gotten along?"

Before she could answer, their drinks came out to them. The waitress put Weirdlee's wine and the men's two draft beers on the table before each of them, then departed again.

Weirdlee took up where Nicks left off.

"I've talked with a few people Henneger used to work with at Pioneer Valley Contractors, and also a few he used to hang out with at a restaurant over in Hadley, on the main road, there." She took a sip of her wine. "There's a guy at one of his Northampton haunts that I'm talking with, as well."

"Okay," Nicks said. "Let's get through the original interview list before we start questioning other people. Henneger knows we're on his ass, though, so he might start trying to make sure people keep their mouths shut—or remember their stories."

"Like Lisa Saunders," Weirdlee said.

"Exactly."

Nicks looked to Fielding. "Ask the state police if they can put an unmarked car on Ms. Saunders—just in case things get nasty with Henneger."

"He'll spot the tail. Or she will," Fielding said.

"That's okay," said Nicks. "I just don't want her getting snuffed out before we bring her in." He drummed his fingers on the table then, thinking of other considerations. "I'd like to go over the timing of everything that went on that weekend, too. Saturday night in particular. The police report says Henneger told the police the two women were gone by the time he got home that night. That had to have been sometime after nine or nine-thirtyish, at least, since Suzanne Kerch was on the phone with a friend right about then."

"Well, we're assuming he lied, right?" asked Fielding.

Nicks shook his head. "Doesn't matter. We can't base anything on assumptions." He looked at Weirdlee. "He was at a bar that night, he said, and then went home from there."

Weirdlee nodded. "That would be O'Brien's Pub."

"Right. See if anyone there remembers him being there that night."

Weirdlee tilted her head and winced at that. She recalled her second visit to O'Brien's, when she'd received a less than friendly welcome from the locals there—all of whom seemed more eager to watch out for their friend, Henneger, than help out the law. "I think I've about worn out my welcome there, Samuel. They're looking at *us* as the bad guys, unfortunately."

Nicks rolled his eyes at the first name reference. "Call me Sam, if you have to, please."

She winked at him. "Okay. Sure thing, *Sam*."

"Anyway," Nicks continued, "if they're not cooperating with us, then we'll have to find out some other way of determining when he actually got home."

Weirdlee gave a slow nod as she pondered something. "I...think I've still got one friend there, at least. The guy I mentioned. I might be able to get something more out of him if I can catch him outside of the bar."

"All right then," said Nicks. "Give it a shot."

Shortly thereafter, their dinner arrived, and the agents talked shop for a little while longer before calling it an early night.

9

The Devil and the Witch

Henneger woke up in the morning, hungover as usual from the night before. He still wore yesterday's clothing—a dirty t-shirt and worn pair of jeans—and nearly knocked over a half-filled can of beer from his nightstand as he dragged himself out of bed.

His head pounded. He'd taken down ten beers, at least, while carousing with his friends at O'Brien's Pub. They'd ragged on him pretty damned good for a while, teasing him about the FBI sniffing around for him. But most of them also voiced support for their long-time drinking buddy. The Feds were a bunch of jack-booted thugs, after all, always trying to screw the so-called undesirables of society. Henneger, meanwhile, was a local guy and a friend, and they weren't about to turn on one of their own. That much was for sure.

Still, he was fired up about the whole situation.

The police had nothing on him, he was certain, and the FBI appeared to be just going through the motions of double-checking everything the cops had done before.

They got nothin', he assured himself.

He pulled off his jeans, shirt, and briefs and hopped into the shower. Under the relaxing streams of hot water, he lathered himself up and washed away a full day and night's worth of sweat and grime. The teasing and smack talk he'd endured the night before came back to him. If only they knew who they were talking to, he mused, he wondered how many of them would even want to be in the same room with him. He smiled as he pondered the question.

Rinsing soap from his face, Henneger then doused his head fully under the shower to soak his thinning hair. He poured a fair amount of shampoo into his hand then and lathered up his head.

Suzanne, that miserable bitch, he recalled, had had it coming to her. He'd made up his mind about that a long time ago.

The night she approached him with that letter from the court in-hand, telling him she'd been subpoenaed as a witness in an investigation, and that she'd tell the cops everything they wanted to know about his drug dealing if she didn't get her way, was just the last straw for him. And when he pounded her head onto that hardwood floor in the hallway—over and over again—he remembered how truly satisfying the feeling had been for him.

No, he held no remorse in his mind at all for having given her what she endured that night. Not anymore. Just a profound sense of relief that he'd actually gotten away with it.

Goddamn, he marveled, *how many people could get away with something that?*

It was the demise of Becky, though, that still haunted him through the years. She'd heard the screaming and pounding going on, and she was yelling, herself, from the bottom of the stairs.

There was only one thing he could do, given the situation.

He came down the stairs, to where she stood in the first floor hallway. She was still screaming at him—a look of rage fixed on her young, innocent face.

"What did you do to my mother!" she yelled.

There was no emotion on Henneger's own face as he stalked up to her. And when he grabbed hold of her by her skinny little neck, he remembered quite vividly the sudden change in her expression, going from rage to absolute horror. He forced himself upon her then and shoved her to the floor. She thrashed and punched and shoved as best she could from underneath him, but she was far too weak for such a fight to go on for very long. As his grip around her neck tightened, her expression grew distraught, and he could hear her whimpering and see her eyes welling up with tears. Such a tragic look of profound sadness she had, as if she were begging him with her eyes—for she could not speak—to please not end her young life right there and then. He watched and listened to her all the while, even as her choked cries grew weaker and the last few horrible seconds of her life went by until, finally, even as he looked into her tear-soaked eyes, he saw them drift off to a still lifelessness, gazing ahead at nothing but the great beyond.

He kept a firm grip on her for a moment longer then, squeezing her neck extra tightly, just to be sure, before finally relaxing his hold.

"Becky?" he whispered to her. "You there, girl?"

She was gone.

After his shower, Henneger got dressed and fixed a cup of black instant coffee to go along with a leftover doughnut he'd saved from the day before. Sitting in his kitchen and enjoying his breakfast, he went over, once more, the steps he'd taken that allowed him to elude justice for so long.

First, the wrapping of the bodies. Then, the phone call to Lisa. Then, after she arrived, hauling them out to the van, followed by that long, desperate drive, without being seen. He'd hatched his story while on the road, and, upon his return, was relieved to see his house and that of his neighbors still dark and peaceful. He cleaned Suzanne's blood off the hallway floor and picked up a few things.

Finally, then, the next night, he went back out to visit Lisa, and the two finished the job.

Did he miss anything? Anything the Feds might catch, after all?

No, he told himself. They'd have been there, already, if he'd screwed something up.

His breakfast finished, Henneger picked up his car keys and made for the door. *Another day, another dollar.* He opened the door and stepped outside.

"Good morning," came a greeting from across his front yard.

Henneger looked off to see two well-dressed men getting out of a red Chevy Impala parked at the curb. The guy who'd called out to him wore dark sunglasses to shield the stark rays of the early morning sun. He walked around from the driver's side to approach Henneger's front walk. His partner joined him there.

"Mr. Henneger?" he asked.

Henneger eyed both men suspiciously. He answered the first one, "Maybe."

The man with the sunglasses pulled out an ID out from his back pocket and showed it to him. "I'm Special Agent Nicks, with the FBI," he said. He motioned to his partner. "This is Special Agent Fielding."

Henneger put up a halting hand as he started up the walkway towards his van, parked in the driveway. "Hold up, man. Don't be coming onto my property."

Nicks and Fielding stopped at the front of the walkway.

"We'd just like to ask you a couple of questions, Mr. Henneger," said Nicks.

"Yeah? You got a fuckin' warrant?"

Nicks glanced to Fielding, then looked back at Henneger. "Not sure we need a warrant just to talk with you, sir."

Henneger continued to his van. "You guys are harassing me," he snarled, pointing to them. "You and that fuckin' red-headed bitch."

Nicks feigned innocence. "How are we harassing you, sir? We're just looking into an old case we've been assigned to, that's all. You know, the missing Kerch women?"

Henneger stopped at his driver-side door. He glared at the two agents. "I know all about it. I answered all your fuckin' questions ten years ago. Leave me the fuck alone."

Nicks rested his hands on his hips. "Mr. Henneger, aren't you the least bit curious about what happened to Suzanne Kerch after all these years?"

"Nope," Henneger replied, getting into his van.

Nicks walked over to the left side of the short driveway, there to talk to Henneger as he started up his vehicle.

"Mr. Henneger," he began.

Henneger growled at him, "I told you to stay off my property."

Nicks shook his head ruefully. "Gosh, you know, sir, you could at least fake some sense of despair or something."

"Fuck her," Henneger shot back. "She took off on me. What do you want me to do? Cry tears? You guys have been bustin' my balls ever since. Now back off, before I get a lawyer and sue all your asses."

He gunned his van in reverse then to get out of the driveway. Skidding onto the street, he shifted it into drive, then sped off down the road, leaving Nicks and Fielding standing there watching him.

Fielding walked over to Nicks.

"Well," he said to him despondently, "that was a short interview."

Nicks pursed his lips. He eyed Henneger's van as it rounded a corner in the distance.

"Yeah..." he mulled. Then he started back to their car.

"What'll we do if he ain't talkin' to us?" Fielding asked, walking after him.

"We'll just have to go by his original police report," said Nicks.

Both men got back to their car and climbed inside.

"Let's go visit the Northampton PD," Nicks went on. "I want check on some things and take a look at their records—see if any of Mr. Henneger's friends have gotten themselves into any trouble through the years."

He started up the car, and Fielding looked at him curiously.

"Why is that important?"

Nicks looked off down the road as he answered. "That guy's got a lot of loyal friends, Agent Fielding." He checked his rearview mirror for traffic before pulling away from the curb. "I'm thinking about that woman who rented Henneger's house after he went to prison."

"Saunders?" Fielding asked.

"Yeah, her. It's possible that that whole story of hers, about her needing a cheap place to stay, is all a bunch of bullshit. And in that case, I can assume they had some kind of relationship going on—platonic or not, I don't know. But we'll need to dig a little bit in that direction."

"So maybe she has a record?" Fielding asked.

Nicks gave nod. "Possibly. We can check on that."

He turned onto Route 9 West, heading them back toward downtown Northampton.

"After we get done talking to the police," he continued, "we'll head back to the hotel and change. No sense in us stomping around the dump in our good clothes."

"Right," Fielding said. "I printed out an archive map of the landfill, too. Looks like the area they used back in 2004 was right about in the center of the place. There could be a whole lotta shit in there, partner. Hell, maybe we'll find some bodies we ain't lookin' for."

Nicks turned to him and grinned. "Maybe so."

****

Sandy Whiting drove out to the Northampton landfill on Glendale Road at just before 11:00 AM. The landfill itself had closed two years before, and the property's front service area was currently used only as a recycling center. The center on this day, though, was closed due to the FBI's search operation, so Whiting only made it as far as the center's closed gate before being stopped by a state trooper posted there. Getting out of her car, she got into a heated argument with the trooper before Agent Fielding—standing with Nicks atop the nearside of the landfill's vast, landscaped dome—spotted her and called out for the officer to let her in.

Whiting got back into her car and drove inside the gate. Parking her car in the center's lot, she then marched up the grassy dome.

Approaching the two agents, she saw that both men were now dressed casually—Fielding in dark slacks and a golf shirt, Nicks in blue jeans and a gray t-shirt. Dirt swirled about them in the warm summer air as two backhoes dug up earth along a wide track just behind them. Working ahead of the backhoes, the Guardian GPR team swept around in a series of back-and-forth patterns along the grassy dome's eastern side.

"You searching the whole landfill?" Whiting asked the men as she came up to them.

Nicks looked off to the GPR team. "No, ma'am. Just the area they used ten years ago."

Whiting waved her hands around. "He could have buried them anywhere out here."

Nicks conceded that. "That's possible, Mrs. Whiting. But we need to start from the most likely areas, first. If they're here, then whoever put 'em here would have probably looked for a spot where he'd know they'd get buried right off—and deep."

Whiting shook her head as she eyed the area. "Well, you guys know your business." She looked at Nicks. "You think he'd drive out here on his own to bury them here?"

"Henneger?"

"Yeah, him. Is there anyone else?"

"I'm not putting anything past anyone, yet, Mrs. Whiting."

Fielding added, "He coulda come out here on his own, at night. But the gate woulda been locked. He'da had to have climbed over the property fence, here, and I ain't seein' that with two bodies—" he stopped himself, remembering who he was talking to. "Sorry, ma'am."

Whiting walked up to Fielding and looked at him squarely. She said to him, "What? You think I haven't been out here, walking around myself? You think I don't know what I might find?" She turned away to look off at the grassy dome around them. "I used to come out here a couple days a week. I used dig through all the garbage, all the maggots and all that other shit..." her voice trailed off. "I'd come out here, and I knew what I'd see if I found them." She turned back around to face the two agents, and she stepped closer to Nicks. She bit her lip as she looked at him, and Nicks could see, once more, the fragile woman he'd met that past Saturday. "My sister and my niece are *dead*," she said to him. "And their bodies are the only things that'll put away the son of bitch who killed them. You think I don't know that?"

Nicks stood there stoically. He'd seen such heartache expressed many times before.

"I know you do," he said to her.

Whiting wiped away tears from her eyes. "You know what I need?" she asked Nicks in a weak voice.

"No ma'am," he replied.

She sniffled, and she recovered herself as best she could, even managing a fragile smile. "I could use a hero right about now. You know?"

Nicks understood that, and gave her a nod. "Yes, ma'am."

****

Route 9 in downtown Northampton bisected the little city, going east-to-west. While leaving downtown and traveling eastbound, the route dipped under a north-south railroad trestle. From there, the way opened up to a more suburban environment where the front lawns and well-manicured parking lots of various businesses lined the street along either side.

Just a few dozen yards beyond the railroad trestle on the south-facing side of the route was Pasta Leone's, an Italian restaurant featuring a large outdoor patio for dining. On the opposite side of the street from this, across an intersection, was another, smaller eatery called The Corner Bistro.

Inside this latter venue, Fred Duncan sat on a small wooden bench eating a ham and cheese sandwich with chips on the side and sipping on a root beer in between. He sat in such a way as to be able to look out from the bistro's large display window that faced the street. His table was just a small, square thing, barely big enough for two diners, with another chair set to the right of his own.

Taking a healthy bite out of his sandwich, Fred's eyes wandered about the scenery outside. His vision was poor after just a few feet, but even so, he could still make out the color of peoples' hair and how they dressed. He watched as a regular stream of cars passed by in either direction through the intersection and pedestrians went about their business along the sidewalks on either side of the street. Then, on the far sidewalk, he first caught sight of someone he thought for sure he recognized:

The lady FBI agent!

He squinted, keeping his eyes on her as she walked purposefully along, sharp-looking in her black skirt suit and matching jacket. She wore her dark, thick-rimmed sunglasses under the mid-day sun, and carried her small purse slung over her left shoulder. Her long, dark red hair distinguished her from the others around her.

Fred watched the pretty agent as she stopped at the curb. There, she waited for a break in the traffic, then walked across the street. Once on the nearside sidewalk, she continued on her way, approaching the bistro as she went along.

Fred imagined she might look inside the big window as she walked by, and he smiled, anticipating waving to her if she did. But her gaze never wavered from the sidewalk ahead of her as she walked past the window from where he looked. He felt a little let down, then, as he watched her go by, even knowing Henneger would kick his ass if he ever found out he'd been talking to her again.

Still, she sure was pretty to look at.

Then, something incredible happened. The FBI girl stopped at the corner entrance to the bistro, and she opened the door.

She was coming inside!

His adrenaline pumping again, Fred quickly wiped his mouth with a hand and then checked his shirt for any fallen crumbs. He brushed them off.

Agent Weirdlee walked into the place. She removed her

sunglasses as she walked up to the ordering bar. Her gaze stayed on the large, wall-mounted menu behind the bar as she eyed her choices. A server came up to her and waited.

"A...mixed salad," Weirdlee ordered, "and...I guess an iced tea. Unsweetened."

The server took down her order and then went off to fetch it.

Weirdlee tucked her sunglasses into her left jacket pocket. After that, she glanced around at her surroundings and—quickly spotting Fred sitting at his table—warmly greeted him.

"Freddy," she said to him with a smile. "Small world."

Small world it was indeed, but it wasn't *that* small. For Weirdlee's arrival was not the chance encounter Fred believed it to be. Rather, the special agent knew, in her own way, right where to find him.

Fred, meanwhile, was in absolute heaven. Fuck Henneger telling him not to talk to her anymore. "Hi there," he replied eagerly.

Weirdlee waited a moment longer for her salad and iced tea to arrive. She pulled out a credit card from her purse and paid for it, then picked up her order and turned around to glance about at the surrounding tables. Her eyes, though, quickly settled on Fred again.

"Mind if I join you?" she asked him.

Fred was *higher* than heaven!

"Sure," he gushed. He brushed off a few breadcrumbs from the tabletop and then pulled his own sandwich wrapper to the side to make room for her. "Plenty of room."

Weirdlee smiled and walked over. She set her salad and drink on the table and took a seat next to Fred.

Fred ogled her as she sat down. Her moist red lipstick, he saw, matched perfectly with her hair, and he took special note of her legs as she crossed them.

"So," Weirdlee said to him, fully aware of his wandering eyes. "Is this a regular place of yours, too?"

Fred looked at her nervously. "Uh, yeah. I like to come here for lunch, anyway."

Weirdlee started in on her salad as she continued.

"You get set in your ways," she said, "regular places and habits and such, I suppose."

"Yeah, I guess so."

"Of course," Weirdlee said, taking a sip of her iced tea, "then there's those times when something important happens on a particular night. You can remember a conversation you had that night just because you can picture it all so clear in your mind. You know what I mean?"

Fred squinted, having to think a bit on that one. "*Ehh*...I dunno."

Weirdlee assured him then: "I'm willing to bet you could remember a conversation from a few years ago, if something important happened on that same night."

Fred shook his head. "Nooo, can't do that. Can't even remember who I talked to *last* night," he chuckled.

"You were talking to John Henneger last night," Weirdlee said, her tone suddenly turned serious.

Fred gulped and looked at her.

"Sandy Whiting, Suzanne Kerch's sister, was there last night, too," she sad.

Fred tensed up—he wasn't supposed to be talking to the FBI girl!

"Yeah," he said nervously. "Earlier."

"Mrs. Whiting misses her sister very much, Fred. You can understand that, right?"

Fred stared at her, trembling. "I don't know nothin'," he muttered.

Then, in a stern voice, Weirdlee said something quite coldly to him.

"Suzanne Kerch is dead, Fred."

Fred shook his head. "I dunno. Maybe she took off."

"She's *dead*. And you know her daughter's dead, too."

Fred went pale. This wasn't fun anymore!

He muttered, "I dunno."

Weirdlee reached over and put a hand on his own. "Fred," she said softly to him, her friendly demeanor returning, "somebody killed Suzanne and Becky Kerch. You know that's true. And we both know who likely did it."

"I'm sorry, but I don't know nothin'."

She looked at him sincerely. "You know, Fred, we're the good guys, you and I, no matter what anyone else says."

Fred stared down at Weirdlee's slim, pretty hand upon his own much older, uglier one. Her touch was so warm and gentle. He couldn't remember the last time a woman touched him that way. He missed it so!

"Fred," Weirdlee said, getting his attention. He looked at her as she spoke to him. "I'm not here to lie to you. My colleagues and I are here to find and arrest the man who killed the Kerches. We are going to do this, if we can. But we need your help."

Fred, however, felt helpless.

"I don't know anything. I'm serious."

"I want to talk to you about the night the Kerches disappeared," Weirdlee said. "That Saturday night."

Fred shook his head. "Shit, I can't remember that."

"Yes, you can."

"It was ten years ago—I can't."

"You remember all the talk that went on that week, don't you—after the women went missing?"

Fred tried to think, but his nerves were getting to him. He glanced all around the bistro, suddenly anxious about someone seeing him there with the FBI girl.

"I don't know. It was a long time ago."

Weirdlee took her hand away from his. She grabbed her fork and jabbed it into her salad. "Okay," she said, getting back to eating her lunch, "it made the news by the end of the week, though—by that following Saturday, anyway."

"Yeah, I remember that, I guess."

"Wasn't Mr. Henneger your friend back then?"

Fred shrugged. "Well, yeah."

"Didn't you talk to him? Didn't people ask him what happened?"

"I guess so, yeah. He said they took off on him."

"He didn't tell you about them fighting or anything?"

"Shit," Fred swore. "They fought all the time."

"Did they?"

"Sure. She didn't like him going out drinking all the time."

"And he went out every Saturday night back then?"

Fred laughed. "Still does."

"He was out on the Saturday they disappeared, too?"

"Probably."

"He told the police he was."

"Yeah—he was. I remember. And he told me, when he got home, they were gone."

"He told you that?"

"Yeah."

"Were *you* there that night, Fred?"

Fred squinted at first, trying to recall. Then suddenly, his face lit up as the fog of time lifted from mind. "I *was* there. We were watching the Super Bowl—a replay from the one we won that year."

"The Super Bowl?"

"Yeah. The Pats. They'd won it that year, and they were showing the game that night."

"You remember that?"

Fred nodded eagerly. "Yep."

"When was the game on, Fred? Was it earlier or later?"

"Uhh..." Fred considered, "I think it started at, like, six-thirty or seven o'clock."

Weirdlee calculated the time of an NFL game in her head. Even minus the Super Bowl's halftime show—a replay of the game most likely wouldn't bother with it—she didn't like what it came out to. "So...it lasted until after ten o'clock?"

"Uhh, yeah, something like that, I think."

"And John stayed there till the end," she suggested.

Fred crimped his face, trying to recall. "No, I don't think he did."

New hope for Weirdlee. "He didn't?"

"Nah. He said something like, um, we'd seen it before, anyway, so what the fuck? We knew how it ended, you know? What a game it was!"

"So he didn't stay for the whole game that Saturday," Weirdlee pressed.

Fred thought it over. "Nnno...he left before it ended."

Weirdlee leaned forward in her chair. She was all done eating. "Fred," she said, "what time do you think he left the bar that night?"

That was a hard question for him to answer. He mulled it over in his head, but shit, what *time?*

"I dunno. I can't remember that."

"Was it before or after halftime?"

More thinking over.

"Uhhh, I think it was right at halftime. No—wait. Just a couple minutes before."

Weirdlee smiled at him. "Really?"

"Yeah," said Fred, and he laughed. "I remember that. He was bitchin' about the game and knowing what was gonna happen and all. Then they had a time out just before halftime, and he said 'I'm outta here'."

"Did he really?"

Fred was quite pleased with himself. "Yeah, he did."

"So," Weirdlee calculated, "we're talking about maybe...eight o'clock, eight-thirty then?"

Fred shrugged. "I guess so, maybe. I don't remember what time it was."

Weirdlee let the matter go. Checking the actual time of the replayed game would be easy enough. The important thing was that Henneger had left before halftime, which, if he went directly home from the bar—as he stated in his police report that he did—means he would have been home before, or at the same time, Suzanne had her phone call with a friend.

"Fred," she said, "do you think you could write that down for me—what you just said? Maybe stop by the police station and fill out a statement?"

Fred looked at her, shocked. "Hell, no!"

"Why not?"

"I don't want nothin' to do with this!"

Weirdlee's expression grew suddenly stern. She said to Fred in a hushed voice, "You already *are* a part of this. You have important information, Fred, and you're keeping it to yourself. Two women are dead, and you know in your heart who killed them. I know you do."

Fred looked at her, terrified. The FBI girl had tricked him into talking! She had fooled him! And now, what was John going to do to him after he found out?

He pleaded to her in a meek voice, "I don't wanna get in trouble."

Weirdlee's own tone mellowed, and she looked at him in a more friendly way. "You're not in any trouble, Fred. We can help you. We can protect you if you're afraid. But you have to help us, first."

Fred swallowed, considering what to do. He was

crossing a very frightening line. He had promised Henneger that he wouldn't betray him, and now there he was, about to quite possibly do just that.

He shrugged uneasily, unable to make up his mind. "I dunno. I'll think about it."

Weirdlee nodded. "Okay, Fred. I'm going to trust you on this. You go ahead and think about it."

Just then, out of the corner of her eye, Weirdlee saw the man she'd hoped not to see for another half an hour or more. It was Henneger, and he was getting out of his van across the intersection, just in front of the Italian restaurant Pasta Leone's.

Dammit.

He was early.

She looked at Fred. "Gotta go, Fred." She got up from her seat and gathered up her salad plate and iced tea.

Fred moved to join her. "Okay, me too."

She stopped him. "No-no. Stay here. Finish your sandwich."

Fred looked down at his sandwich. It had a few bites left to it, still. "Oh, I can finish it quick."

"No, take your time," she said to him. She set her plate back down then, and she reached into her purse to fetch out a business card. She set it on the table in front of Fred. "If you do decide to help us out, you let me know. We can protect you."

Fred eyed the card, and nodded. "Okay."

"In the meantime," Weirdlee went on, picking up her plate again, "I'll just go ahead and let the police know you might stop in. That way they'll be expecting you if you do show up."

Weirdlee smiled once more at Fred before stepping away. She brought her nearly empty salad plate to the trash and dumped it. Then she took a long, last sip of her iced tea and likewise deposited it there.

Fred smiled at her as he watched her leave the bistro. It was a nervous smile, though, filled with misgiving over everything going on.

Could he actually do what she wanted him to do, he wondered. Could he actually betray the trust of a friend?

He looked back down at her business card.

He was very much afraid he would.

Weirdlee walked across the intersection to get to the south side of the street, just in front of Pasta Leone's. She glanced behind her to make sure Fred had stayed inside the bistro, then she turned and looked inside the window of the restaurant. There, Henneger was paying for a take out order—a grinder. She waited for him to finish paying, and then, seeing him grab his order and head for the door, she started off on her own way, casually walking toward the train trestle underpass.

Henneger made it to the door and grabbed the latch. As he opened it, he looked outside, his eyes briefly wandering about the scenery, seeing the traffic on the street and the pedestrians on the far sidewalk, and then, off to his right...

The FBI girl!

Son of a bitch!

He tossed his grinder into his van and then broke into a sprint down the sidewalk after her.

Weirdlee, meanwhile, had made it under the trestle and, still walking at her leisure, turned left to go up a flight of steps that led to the top of the bridge. The railroad trestle spanning Route 9 actually consisted of two bridges set side-by-side—one for the railway tracks that traversed it, and a second one for pedestrian traffic. The steps Weirdlee had gone up were set in between them.

Henneger raced to the steps himself and scrambled up

their flight, his eyes eagerly looking to the top, but seeing no sign of the woman he pursued.

At the top of the trestle, with the railroad tracks to his left and the pedestrian walkway to his right, he again glanced around for his quarry.

Nothing.

An older couple came walking towards him along the walkway. He watched them as they passed by him and continued over the trestle, heading north. Looking beyond them, to the other side of the trestle, he still saw no sign of the FBI woman.

A few other people came along in either direction then, out for their daytime stroll.

That fucking bitch, he fumed. She had ditched him again!

He turned back around, and he looked off once more to the southerly route, where the pedestrian path—actually a paved route that bicyclists also used—continued along a wide, flat berm. To the path's left, the train tracks ran parallel, going off into the distance.

He moved ahead.

Off to the right of the path, the rear side of a long, multi-storied building took up much of the view. The building's second story was level with the berm, and, located at regular intervals along its length, the rear entrances of businesses whose storefronts were on the front side of the building poked out. Each rear entrance hosted a well manicured, neatly cut parcel of lawn facing the pathway. Some of the entrances also had shrubbery growing at either side of their doors.

Farther ahead of Henneger as he stalked along, another building—this one a large structure that took up the space between the pathway and the railroad tracks—came up on his left. This was the city's former train station, currently vacant and in between business tenants. He paid that building little mind, though, as his eager glare scanned the grassy little backyards of the building on his right as he passed each one by.

Nothing, though.

He glanced over at the other building, then, only to see no one there, either.

Where the fuck could she have gone to?

Finally, approaching the corner of the building on his right, Henneger came upon another, narrow flight of steps that led back down to street level. He peered down them, ready to descend their length.

"Good afternoon," greeted a woman from off to his right.

He snapped his eyes to her—there to see none other than the FBI woman herself!

"Looking for me?" she asked him.

"What the fuck?" he swore, surprised.

How, he wondered, could he have possibly missed her there, standing right out in the open as she was on the last of those well-manicured little lawns?

He strode up to her.

"You followin' me, lady?"

She glanced to her left, eyeing the trestle, and then looked back at him. "I believe you're the one doing the following, Mr. Henneger," she said, her Boston accent obvious to his ear.

He scowled at her. "Yeah, you sure as hell know my name, don't you?"

Standing tall before her, he kept a menacing pose. He couldn't help, though, but admire her good looks—giving the woman a once-over and then letting his eyes linger upon reaching her partially unbuttoned blouse.

"You're that FBI girl who's been going around here asking questions about me," he said, raising his eyes to hers.

"Mmmm," Weirdlee purred. "You sound upset, Mr. Henneger."

"Fuck you," he shot back, not allowing her beauty to sway him. "And fuck your partners, too. Going around digging up shit, tryin' to set me up for something I didn't do."

Weirdlee gave him a curious look. "I'm not sure that's the case, Mr. Henneger. We're not in the business of setting up innocent people."

Unexpectedly then, Henneger reached out for Weirdlee's shoulder, and she immediately took a step back. He smiled at her, pleased with himself, while noting as well that she displayed no sign of worry in her expression. He said to her, "Just checkin' to see if you're real, that's all."

She smiled coyly back at him. "You think I'm a figment of your imagination, do you?"

Henneger replied, "Thought you were a ghost at first. But I think I got it wrong. You're more like a fuckin' witch. That's what you are, ain't it? I mean a *real* one."

Weirdlee laughed airily at that. "Oh, Mr. Henneger. Tell me you don't believe in all that hocus pocus."

Henneger jabbed a finger at her. "You're a fuckin' witch, all right. And I bet you're from Salem, too, you fuckin' witch."

"Really?" Weirdlee laughed.

"Yeah. And you know what they do to witches, don't you?"

Weirdlee's innocent smile left her. She eyed Henneger sternly, saying to him, "What's that, Mr. Henneger?"

He sneered at her. "They burn 'em."

Weirdlee kept her glare.

"No," she said to him. "They hang them, actually."

"Oh really?" Henneger replied. "Thanks for the

correction. I figured you'd know."

Weirdlee eased her mood then. "You're a superstitious sort of man, aren't you, Mr. Henneger? Believe in the tooth fairy, too?"

Henneger laughed. "Yeah, sure." He gave her another very obvious, raised eyebrow once-over. "If they're as hot as you are, I do."

Weirdlee smirked at him. "You'd best be on your way, Mr. Henneger. Nothing to see here."

Henneger, though, wasn't finished just yet. He took another step closer to her, so that he stood directly before her.

He said to her, "Never had me a witch before." Then he looked again to her unbuttoned blouse, and he grinned. "Maybe someday."

He turned and stepped away then, and Weirdlee kept her eyes on him as he walked back the way he'd come. Only after he'd descended the stairs at the trestle did the special agent relax her composure.

Mr. Henneger, she realized, was quite perceptive, after all.

****

It was 2:00 PM at the Northampton landfill, and by this time the backhoes had been joined by an excavator to continue their work. Special Agents Nicks and Fielding had just returned from their lunch break, and presently they stood beside their rented Impala at the landfill's front parking lot. A state trooper was there as well, posted at the landfill's gate. Sandy Whiting, meanwhile, had found a spot for herself atop of the landfill's dome, and she stood there quietly on her own observing the excavation. The television media, as expected, had also made their appearance, arriving earlier that morning in order to file their reports in time for the midday news segments. Other reporters came and left throughout the day. As before, Nicks directed the press to the local authorities for comment.

Nicks had also conferred with the Northampton police regarding any arrest record Lisa Saunders might have with them. They told him that she'd turned up clean, however. Meanwhile, two of Henneger's drinking buddies did have drug-related arrests on file. Both, however, turned out to be minor pot possession charges, and so nothing that would warrant further investigation. On another matter— regarding whether Henneger had owned a boat while living in Hadley—they'd also come up empty. There was no record of him having a boat registered, and no one they interviewed recalled him ever having one.

Presently, a Massachusetts State Police cruiser drove through the front gate and pulled into the parking lot, parking next to the agents. Two troopers got out of the vehicle, and the driver, Lieutenant Jim Massey, approached the FBI men.

"We just finished our search of Elwell island," he said to Nicks, speaking of a small, forested islet in the Connecticut River tucked between Northampton and Hadley, just north of the Calvin Coolidge Bridge. "Nothing to report there."

Nicks gave him a nod. "Thanks."

Massey looked off to the landfill dome, there spotting Sandy Whiting perched at its top. "That the Whiting woman up there?"

Nicks answered, "Yep."

The lieutenant turned to him, frowning. "The Northampton PD told me she started some trouble in town last night."

"Yeah," Nicks replied.

"Nothin' big," added Fielding, standing nearby.

"We need to tell her to stay out of this," said Massey. He pointed off to her. "She shouldn't even be up there."

Nicks put his hands on his hips and looked off to Whiting himself. "Oh, she's not interfering with anything we're doing. And if she's getting our guy a little agitated, then good."

"You're endangering her safety, Agent Nicks," Massey said.

Nicks looked at him. "I've been meaning to talk to you about that. I'd like you to put an officer with her until this is all done."

Massey put up a hand. "Now wait a minute. We're already tailing the Saunders woman."

"It's just for today," said Nicks. "I've called our Boston field office and asked for a couple of guys."

"You should tell Mrs. Whiting to go home," Massey said. "There's nothing for her to do out here. We're just wasting manpower."

"I understand your position, Lieutenant," said Nicks, "but bear with me."

Just then, from out on Glendale Road, an old, beat-up van came barreling along. This was none other than John Henneger himself, who'd apparently watched the noontime news and so learned about the landfill search. The FBI men and police lieutenant watched as his speeding van careened into the landfill's driveway and then came to a screeching halt just before the state trooper posted at the gate, who waved frantically for him to stop.

Henneger leaped out of the driver's side, all afury. He ignored the trooper approaching him, and looked off at Nicks and Fielding in the parking lot. "You fuckin' assholes!" he screamed at them. "You got everyone callin' me a murderer! The whole fuckin' town!"

Nicks, Fielding, and Massey all looked back at him, a bit

taken aback.

The trooper nearby Henneger instructed him to back off. Henneger sneered at him. "Fuck off," he said, waving at the driveway. "I'm outside, here."

"Let him be," Massey called out to the trooper. "As long as he stays on that side of the gate."

Henneger marched up closer to the gate, the trooper following in escort. He yelled out at the men inside, "You keep that fuckin' redheaded witch away from me! You hear me? I'll sue all your asses for harassment!" Then he spotted Sandy Whiting atop the landfill dome, and he jabbed a finger at her. "And you keep *that* fuckin' bitch away from me, too! I've had enough of her bullshit!"

Nicks looked casually at the lieutenant. "See? I told you."

"I wonder what Agent Weirdlee did to get him all worked up?" Fielding asked.

Henneger paced back and forth as he continued to spout off. "I been through all this bullshit a dozen times before! Ten fucking years of you assholes hounding me! I am fuckin' tired of it!" He stormed off back toward his van then, pointing at the agents. "I'm getting me a lawyer, and you assholes are gonna pay if you keep it up!"

Reaching his van, he jerked open the driver's door and jumped inside. Firing it up, he yanked the vehicle into reverse and spun it about, kicking up a cloud of dust. Shifting it into forward, he gunned the van out of the driveway and off down Glendale Road, heading back north.

The lawmen stood there watching him speed off.

"News travels fast," said Fielding. "He came all the way out here just for that?"

Nicks pursed his lips, considering. "The man's getting flustered."

Massey, though, had another thought in mind. "He's

getting pissed off, is what he's getting."

Nicks turned around and looked off at the landfill. "Yeah, well, I don't think we're going to find anything here, anyway. He wouldn't have driven out here if he thought we might be waiting for him with a pair of handcuffs."

From down the road, then, a Hadley police cruiser came along. It slowed and turned into the landfill's driveway.

"More company," quipped Massey.

The state trooper at the gate let the cruiser pass, and it came into the lot and parked close to the other cars. Out of it then hopped Hadley Police Chief Towers and Sergeant Banning.

"Thought I'd find you guys here," said Towers in a tired voice, glancing at both Nicks and Fielding.

"Chief," Nicks greeted him. "What's the word?"

"We're done with the transit station," the chief said.

"Good," said Nicks.

"This is all just a waste of time, you know," said Banning. "All we're doing is retracing what we did ten years ago. And do you honestly believe Henneger would stick around if he thought we might dig up those girls somewhere?"

"No, I don't," Nicks replied tersely. "Once we're all caught up with these old searches, though, I want to get started on some new ones."

"*New* ones?" Towers asked.

"What do you mean?" asked Massey, too, sharing the chief's curiosity.

"Look, this guy's been all over the place the past ten years," Nicks explained. "We have to assume there's a possibility he might have taken the bodies on a road trip somewhere. He could have kept them someplace temporarily and then moved them to a more permanent spot later on. He didn't destroy them—I'm pretty sure of that, now. He wouldn't be all pissed off at us if he did. So they're *somewhere*. We're just not looking in the right places." He turned to Towers, saying, "We need to know everything about this guy—who his friends were back in the day, where his other job sites were located. I'd also like to know where he goes to for vacation."

"Vacation?" Towers snarled. "You think he took their remains on vacation with him?"

Nicks answered, "Henneger's a pretty smart guy, Chief. He's not going to dump their bodies just anywhere and then hope for the best. He's going to put them in a spot he knows well enough to be sure they won't be found. He'll have been there before—maybe even lots of times before. Hell, he may *still* go there today."

"Shit," said Fielding. "He coulda dumped them into the ocean, for all we know."

Nicks looked at him. "Let's just hope for our sake he didn't."

Massey took out his smartphone and tapped on his weather app. He studied it, then said, "Well...looks like it's going to pour all day tomorrow. We had plans to do the Hop Brook search over on Station Road. It's a boggy area there, so I suppose since we're gonna get wet anyway, we might as well keep to doing that."

"Yeah," said Nicks. "We can also spend the day catching up on interviews." He turned to Fielding. "Coordinate with Agent Weirdlee. Take care of the remaining people on our list, and I'd also like her to go back and ask some of the people she's already talked to about places Henneger vacations at."

Fielding smiled at him. "*Now* she's our partner, aye, boss?"

Nicks returned his smile. "Ask her nicely."

10

Evening Reflections

Tuesday ended with the investigators wrapping up their search at the landfill. Although he would have preferred things gone better for them, Nicks suspected the day would go just as it had, with no new discoveries.

Fielding drove them both back to the hotel, there to meet up with Special Agent Weirdlee. Fielding and Weirdlee then got together on their own to go over her remaining interviewees, which she then divvied up between them. Fielding asked her how her day had gone, and she said "well enough."

All the while, though, something unsettling stirred inside of Fielding. He recognized that, despite his unyielding love for his wife, he'd felt an attraction to his mysterious colleague that seemed more than just the usual feeling a guy gets when admiring a beautiful woman. She had an alluring hook about her—an emotional, sexual presence that had become more undeniable with each passing day.

Back in the hotel room he shared with Nicks, Fielding lay on his bed, still dressed, quietly mulling over the personal predicament he found himself in. Nicks was out of the room, so for the moment he wrestled with his situation in solitude.

Weirdlee had never given him any indication that she shared his interest or physical attraction. In fact, if anything, she seemed quite dismissive of his presence whenever they were together with Nicks. Perhaps, then, it was simply the way she carried herself, he surmised. She was, after all, a vibrant young woman—he guessed her to be no more than twenty-six years of age. Yet she also had a confidence about her that seemed well beyond her years. She was a focused woman—a university undergrad, he recalled—and Fielding figured her upbringing must have been at least stable enough for her to excel in her studies.

But why all the secrecy? Who could she be, and from where, that it mattered so much to keep it all hidden away?

Fielding himself had come to the Criminal Investigation Division from the Bureau's Cyber Division. As he lay there thinking then, he recalled that he still had a few friends there with favors owed to him. He fetched his smartphone from his bedside dresser, and checked the time display. It read 7:35 PM. Not too late, he figured, to make a phone call. He tapped the display and scrolled through his contacts list. Spotting *Kevin Barnes*, he selected the name and tapped the green phone icon.

Three rings went by, and then a pick up. "Barnes, here. What's shaking, Danny boy?" said Barnes, alerted by his own phone's caller ID.

Fielding smiled. It was good to hear a friendly voice from the past.

"Barnes, ol' pal of mine," he chirped, "how's it goin' in DC these days?"

"We're managing, Danny. Same ol' shit, you know? How's your Big Apple assignment going so far?"

Fielding laughed. "I'll let you know the next time I'm there, buddy. They got us up in Massachusetts these days."

"Massachusetts? What's going on up there?"

"Aww, it's just a cold case the assistant director wants us to look into."

"An interstate job?"

"Nope. Local missing persons. Two girls—a mom and

her daughter." Fielding got to the point, then. "Hey, listen, ol' buddy, that's not what I'm calling you about. I've got a favor to ask ya. You know you owe me a couple, right?"

"Oh, Jesus. Calling me out, are you?"

"Gotta getcha before ya forget."

"Yeah," Barnes laughed, "I know how it is. What can I do for you then?"

"Okay, here's the deal. Me and my partner got us a sidekick from Operations. She's a young thing—maybe in her mid-twenties. But she's kind of a mystery girl, you know?"

"Yeah, sure, I know. What's the matter? Not coming on to your charms, is she?"

"Shit, man," Fielding scoffed playfully, "you know I'm a married man."

"Yeah? So? What's she look like?"

"My wife?"

"The *girl*, you freak."

"Look, she's a redhead. My partner and I checked her record just after she came over to us, but it only goes back a couple of years—from her days at Brandeis University. Any time before that, it's classified."

"Brandeis, huh?"

"Yeah."

"Well, shit, maybe they designed her."

Fielding laughed. "Very funny. I'm serious, though."

"So am I," said Barnes. "Sort of, anyway. Maybe they changed her identity to protect her—like they do in witness protection, you know?"

"Yeah..." Fielding sighed. He rubbed his chin, figuring things over in his head. "Look," he said, "I don't want ya gettin' into any trouble or nothin'. Can you just see what pops up in the tube with a little side door action?"

"Sure, Danny. I think I can do that for ya. I might even

call in a couple favors of my own, if you want to owe me."

"Sure." Fielding smiled. "Anything you can find out for us would be great."

****

Later Tuesday evening, Special Agent Weirdlee wrestled with yet another restless night of uneven sleep. This was a common ordeal for her, whenever she traveled about and found herself in unfamiliar environs. This, furthermore, was her first field assignment with the Bureau, so she had the additional stress of not letting down a team she had only just come to know.

She had no idea how things would turn out with the investigation, and it was an uncomfortable feeling for her not knowing what the future held. In her mind, she pictured Henneger—he, the murderer and the corruptor of all that was good in life—and she saw him for the predator that he surely was. He drew in the innocent and poisoned their minds. It was exactly what he did to Suzanne Kerch, Weirdlee determined, by pulling her into a relationship she could never escape from. And it's what he'd done to so many others afterward, too, as he enlisted their aid—knowingly or not—in slipping away from justice.

She'd reported to Nicks earlier in the evening, telling him of Fred's statement about the timing of Henneger's return back home on that dreadful night. She hoped, in her heart, that Nicks was a capable man. He seemed to be just that, but she couldn't read him very well, which to her was a little odd. She couldn't influence him, either. And that was troubling to her.

Maybe, though, that's why Ledds had put her with him. The man was pure, in both spirit and mind.

She rolled over once more in her bed. Her eyes peered

off into the darkness of her hotel room.

Fielding then came into her mind.

What the hell is the matter with that guy?

The man was constantly eyeing her. Wasn't he married?

Pheromones, she reminded herself then. In all her years, she hadn't been able to completely control their effects on those around her. It was something she would need to take into consideration, though, while working out in the field, where she openly interacted with both friend and foe alike. It was something Ledds had mentioned to her once upon a time, too, but she thought him to be teasing. She should have known he was serious, though. He usually was with her. She wasn't, after all, just your ordinary, average, everyday girl.

Never was.

Growing up, Weirdlee had always been a loner, living in a solitary world of her own construct, almost entirely devoid of the loving warmth of friends or family. The other kids around her teased her or were afraid of her. Most adults kept their distance from her—including her own parents, eventually. The psych doctors who counseled her never knew what to make of her "special situation," and the medical doctors who examined her refused to accept the only possible conclusion for her particular condition—that she was, in fact, entirely different from most others who walked this Earth.

Weirdlee curled herself up in her bed and closed her eyes. *Sleep*, she cajoled herself, so weary from the day.

Rest and be thankful for the morning.

****

Special Agent Weirdlee wasn't the only one having trouble sleeping that Tuesday evening. In her hotel room a few miles down the road, Sandy Whiting had tossed and turned for most of the late night before drifting off to sleep. There then, in the netherworld of slumber, her other life returned to her. It was a past life, of a sort, that both comforted her and tormented her. For it was in that alternate place of her own creation that her dear sister and niece remained still very much alive. They still talked to each other there, and they laughed and shared each other's stories of life, love, and all the silly little dramas that everyday living brings.

"I don't think I want to marry the first guy I go out with," said Becky—still a twelve-year-old in this apparition of her—to her mother and Sandy as the three sat at the breakfast table, oddly set on this morning with both cereal bowls and that evening's dinner of baked ham. (This was a dreamland, after all.)

"Don't rush anything," Sandy said to her. "You've got your whole life ahead of you. And don't let some horned-up boy push you into sex, either. There's plenty of time for that, too."

Becky giggled at that, and Suzanne slapped her sister's hand. "Don't put ideas in her head."

"*Mom,*" Becky protested. "You don't think I think about that stuff?"

"There's a difference between making love and just having sex, Becky," Sandy asserted.

Suzanne frowned at her and shook her head. "It's all just sex, Sandy. Making love is just a state of mind."

Sandy rolled her eyes. "*Ohh,* great."—Her sister could be so crude!

"I want to go to college before I have kids," said Becky. "Have my own life."

Sandy ate her breakfast cereal as she offered her own opinion. "That's what we all say. Then we meet a guy, and it's all downhill from there."

Suzanne laughed. "Ain't *that* the truth!"

Becky's mind wandered off into her own daydreamy thoughts then, and she pondered aloud what she wanted out of life.

"I just want a husband and maybe a couple kids, too. And a nice house."

"What? No apartment in the ghetto?" her mom asked sarcastically. "Aiming high, aren't we, hon?"

Becky leered at her playfully. "Aunt Sandy has a house and kids."

Sandy smiled at that. Yes, she did have a complete life.

"I think I want to be a lawyer," Becky went on, "and help people."

Suzanne slapped her forehead. "Jeezuz, baby. Can you pick something else with a cheaper tuition, please?"

All three ladies laughed at that.

It was just after 2:00 AM when Whiting suddenly awakened, taken away from her place at the breakfast table. She was alone once more, lying in her bed inside of her darkened hotel room. There was no laughter. No voices from the past. No sister. And no sweet niece to counsel. Pulling her covers up to her chin, she shuttered as the reality of the present day struck her coldly. She fell into tears then, heartbroken at the thought of once again having been robbed of her sister and niece.

The same way, it was, that all of her dreams of them ended.

11

Wet Wednesday

Wednesday morning it *poured*. So hard, in fact, the Massachusetts State Police had to hold up their search of the Hop Brook area in south Amherst until after 10:00 AM, when the rain finally let up to a steady light shower. Special Agent Nicks arrived just after 11:00 AM, dressed in jeans, a black golf shirt, and knee-high rubber boots. He ventured into the woods by the brook as the search team, dressed in waders and equipped with hooks and poles, sloshed around the brook and surrounding swampy terrain. A cadaver dog also scampered about, its trainer leading it by an extended leash.

Nicks had gone out there because he appreciated the other lawmen's dedication to getting the job done despite the conditions. He also wanted to scratch this place off, once and for all, as a candidate dumping site. The quicker the better, he thought, as there were other sites to scour.

His relations with the state police and Amherst cops were considerably more businesslike than what he had managed with the Hadley police, with whom a lingering animosity remained. Because of this, he was able to communicate a better sense of urgency with the former, and, as a result, the Amherst police had nearly finished the search of their assigned sites in the countryside as well as two condominium sites in town. The next day, Thursday, the state police would also wrap up their searches of the remaining old sites that had been searched ten years prior.

As for the Hadley police, Chief Towers had informed Nicks that they would only be searching the newly-built Fort River Nature Trail along with the Guardian GPR team sometime on Thursday—and charging the FBI, of course, for both the Guardian team's fee and any overtime for his men.

Nicks stood leaning against a tree, quietly watching the searchers as they trudged through the gurgling brook and surrounding swamp, jabbing their poles into the murky waters and muck. The cadaver dog paddled about in the deeper areas to get along his way. It was rough going, for sure, and hard work for the men. But all necessary, too, Nicks told himself, since they had to be able to report with a high degree of confidence that they'd covered every square inch of ground, just in case they found nothing at all.

The special agent's smartphone buzzed, and he pulled it from his belt holster. Seeing it was Fielding, he tapped the green icon and put the phone to his ear.

"Yeah?"

"Nicks, Fielding here."

"Right. What's up?"

"I just got done interviewing a few people this morning. Some of 'em Agent Weirdlee already talked to, but I asked them about where Henneger likes to go on vacation or whatever."

"Okay. How'd it go?"

"Typical bullshit. Nobody knows nothin', except for one guy who said he likes to go to Loudon, New Hampshire. Guess they got a NASCAR track up there?"

Nicks gave nod. "Yeah. Not sure if that helps us, though. Unless he visits places along the way."

"Well, I talked with Weirdlee, too. She said she's goin' out to see that Lisa Saunders woman where she works at to talk to her some more."

"All right. Have you heard anything from the Boston office yet about some bodies?"

One the other end, Fielding nodded. "Yeah, I did. I swung by the Northampton PD and they said two guys were coming out."

Nicks checked his phone for any new message alerts. There were none. He said to Fielding, "You'd think they'd at least let us know."

"Yeah, well..." Fielding's voice trailed off.

"Listen," said Nicks, "you know if that guy Weirdlee talked to ever showed up to give a statement to the Northampton guys?"

Fielding shrugged. "I dunno."

"Check on that for me, will you?" Nicks asked. "I'm going to be in Amherst for the better part of the day, but I'll be back at the hotel by dinnertime."

"Sounds good. I got a couple more people to interview on my end."

"Okay, have at it. I'll talk to you tonight."

"Right."

Nicks tapped off his phone and returned it to its belt holster. He glanced around at his surroundings—the canopy of trees, the fern-covered ground. The rain, by this time, too, was coming down heavier than before. He looked down then towards the brook, where the men had advanced some ways downstream.

Time to go join 'em, he said to himself, and he trudged off to find a way down the embankment.

****

The rain never let up as Fred Duncan scurried frantically along the sidewalk, his umbrella clutched firmly in his hands. He'd spent the previous couple of hours at O'Brien's, anxiously drinking up the courage to go to the police station just a half mile north from there, in downtown Northampton. Fearing someone might see him, he also opted to hoof it to the station in a slightly indirect route, taking a couple of side streets that led him to the rear of the place, where the open backside of the police garage gave him access to the front entrance of the station on Center Street. Once there, Fred glanced around, quite nervous, as he ascended the steps and then walked inside.

Approaching the desk sergeant's counter in the lobby area, Fred introduced himself to the sergeant on duty and told him why he was there. The sergeant nodded knowingly, then directed Fred to the detective's area. "Leave your umbrella with me."

Reporting to the detective's division, Fred was left alone in an office for more than twenty minutes—a situation that only increased his anxiety—until someone finally came along to escort him to another, more plain room. There, he sat at a square wooden table, joined by two detectives as they took down his statement.

An hour—which seemed like an eternity to Fred—passed as the officers went back and forth with him, asking him to retell different parts of his story or add certain other details. He'd thought he'd gone there merely to write up a simple statement, but this was, much to his duress, turning out to be more like an interrogation. He sat there, confused and emotionally unhinged by all of their knit-picky questioning of him, and very much regretting his decision to go there in the first place.

The whole time, too, he saw no sign of the FBI girl, nor any other Feds.

Finally done with everything, the detectives thanked Fred for his time. A flood of relief came over him then as he got up and walked out of the room.

Jeezuz, he sighed as he walked down the hallway. They'd made *him* feel like he was the one under investigation!

He stopped by the desk sergeant to retrieve his umbrella. "You'll need it," the sergeant said to him. "It's still pouring out there."

Fred walked out of the front entrance and pulled open his umbrella. It was a deluge outside, just as the sergeant had warned. He brought the umbrella over his head and started down the front steps.

"Freddy!" came a whiny voice that he recognized almost right away.

He looked off to his left, over to the sidewalk, there to see Barry Funk walking along, carrying his own umbrella perched over his head.

"Watcha doin' there, boss?" Barry asked, stopping at the foot of the steps. "Ya get arrested or somethin'?"

Fred stopped and glanced back at the station. What was he going to say?

"I, uh..." he started.

Dope!

Barry looked past him at the station's entrance. "You get picked up drunk again, boss?"

"Uhh..." Fred stammered, "Yeah. Picked up again."

Barry shook his head and chuckled, "Whatevah," before starting out again. "See ya at the ol' watering hole, boss," he said—by which he meant their common haunt, O'Brien's Pub, where he and all the others who called that place home knew everyone else's business. And where, quite naturally, Barry would now blab about Fred's business, too.

Fred just stared at him as he walked off.

Son of a bitch!

That Barry, he knew, would tell anyone and everyone about how he'd seen him coming out of the police station. And John Henneger, no doubt, was sure to get word of it, too!

Shaking uncontrollably in the downpour, Fred walked down the last couple of steps before coming to the sidewalk, where he stood for a moment, panicked about what to do next.

In times like these, though, there was rarely any doubt in his mind, really. What, after all, did he always do when his nerves got the better of him?

Time for a few beers!

He stalked away purposefully then, heading down Center Street before turning left onto Masonic Street. At the end of that street, on the right, was a local tavern called Benson's.

And the business card Weirdlee had given him earlier? It never even entered his head.

****

It was 3:00 PM, and a heavy rainfall still drenched the wilds of south Amherst. Nicks had joined the search team in the brook as they scoured the boggy terrain. His knee-high rubber boots turned out to be entirely inadequate for the job, though, as he had long since gone into water deeper than they allowed for. No matter. It didn't appear to bother him at all as he talked with the men, and they to him, about the investigation at hand as well as other cases similar to this one. The policemen found Nicks to be quite experienced and professional, and they appreciated his getting soaked and filthy with them when it really wasn't necessary for him to do so. That showed camaraderie—a trait not always so obvious in the otherwise reserved special agent, but something that showed up in him nonetheless once he settled in with a team.

The meandering Hop Brook followed a southeastward

path as they tracked it upstream and deeper into the forest. The current of the brook was so slow it was barely noticeable, and so moving upstream rather than starting at its head didn't much matter to the searchers. Continuing on its southeasterly route then, the brook eventually snaked closer to the Norwottuck Rail Trail, where the trail and stream then followed alongside each other for some distance southeast before the brook's path took a more southerly route, deeper into the Lawrence Swamp.

The searchers had made it to the Norwottuck Rail Trail when they decided to take a break. An Amherst police SUV came up the trail to meet them there with boxes of doughnuts and a good supply of hot coffee from a local Dunkin' Donuts. The coffee was passed around, and the men stood by the trail for their rest, some with umbrellas to catch a break from the pelting rain.

"Man, I tell you, sir," said a young trooper to Nicks, "I half expect to find *somebody's* body out here, you know? It's just creepy."

Nicks, himself not yet given a coffee, grinned thoughtfully as he gazed into the trees. "You never know," he said to the officer. He gave a nod to the forest. "Tough to get in there, though, with a body. I doubt our guy would take a chance by struggling through all that shit. I suppose someone could have just died out there, though, on his own. That could happen."

"Then what are we out here for, sir?"

Nicks looked at him. "Because you never know." Then he stepped toward the treeline, his eyes scanning the woods. "People can go to a lot of trouble to get rid of a body. I've seen them buried, burned, chopped up. Hell, even eaten."

The trooper cringed at that last mention. "Holy shit."

Nicks glanced back at him. "That's what I said, too."

A state police lieutenant walked over to Nicks, a coffee

in each hand. "Coffee, Special Agent?"

Nicks turned to him. "Sure."

The lieutenant gave him a coffee. "We got about another four hours of good daylight here, considering the clouds up there," he said.

"Okay," Nicks replied. "I'd like to keep going south as far as we can."

"It gets pretty bad out there," the lieutenant said, glancing off to the south. "Nothing but a big swamp—lots of water."

Nicks appeared unbothered by the news. "Yep."

He looked back at the rest of the search team then. "We'll give everyone another ten minutes, then get started again."

The lieutenant sipped his coffee. "Roger that."

The search resumed soon thereafter. Despite the constant rain, and the dark, forbidding clouds overhead, the summer air was warm and comfortable, and the search team made good progress moving southward. Nicks every so often checked his smartphone for text messages. Two came from Fielding, updating him on two more interviews he'd finished. A third came from Weirdlee, providing her own update for him:

On way to c Saunders.

****

"Lisa," said Kathy Nettles, a floor nurse working at the Cooley Dickinson Hospital.

Lisa Saunders looked up from checking a patient's meal schedule displayed on a portable console.

"Someone's here to see you," Nettles said. She put her hand up to the side of her mouth, shielding her lips, and whispered, "FBI."

Saunders' heart leapt to her throat. The very worst of everything suddenly flashed through her mind.

Lightheaded with fear, she answered Nettles in a shaken voice.

"FBI? What'd I do?"

Nettles approached her. "She's in the break area. I didn't ask her what she wanted. She said she'd be just a few minutes."

Saunders nodded nervously. She swallowed, gulping air as she started out.

Waiting in the staff break area, Special Agent Weirdlee sat at a small table. The room itself was small, with cupboards taking up two walls and a long counter spanning the far wall, where a small refrigerator, a microwave, and a coffee maker were set. Three more tables, identical to the one Weirdlee sat at, filled in the rest of the room.

Weirdlee looked over at Saunders as the nurse entered the room.

"Ms. Saunders. Good afternoon."

Saunders saw that it was the same woman she'd talked to at the beginning of the week. The FBI agent presently wore a long, dark gray raincoat over her black skirt suit. Her dark red hair fell freely over her coat, tousled a bit from the weather outside.

"Hi," Saunders answered tensely. "You wanted to see me?"

Weirdlee smiled casually. "Yes. Just a few more questions, Ms. Saunders." She pointed at another chair at her table. "Please, have a seat."

Saunders joined her at the table. "I said I didn't know anything."

"I remember," said Weirdlee. "I'd just like to talk to you about your relationship with Mr. Henneger."

Saunders looked back at her, aghast. "There was no relationship. I told you before, we're just friends. That's all."

"I know, I know," Weirdlee replied with a wave of her hand. "I'd just like to ask you about the man himself, though."

"Well—wha-what about him?"

Weirdlee eyed Saunders, noting her distressed demeanor. "There's no need to be upset, Ms. Saunders."

"I'm not upset."

Weirdlee studied her quietly for a moment, making the woman even more uncomfortable.

"What do you want from me?" Saunders asked. "You keep asking me questions like I'm guilty of something."

Weirdlee shrugged. "We're just trying to clear up some things, Ms. Saunders."

Saunders squirmed in her chair. "You make me nervous, like you're trying to set me up."

Weirdlee gave her a curious look. "That's funny you should say that. I spoke with Mr. Henneger earlier, and he seems to think the same thing."

Saunders gulped. Her eyes never left Weirdlee. "Well, it's what you guys do, right?"

Weirdlee laughed lazily at that—even though, in this case, the woman wasn't far off the mark. "I can assure you, Ms. Saunders, no one's trying to set you up. I just need to ask you a few more questions, and then I'll be on my way."

Saunders slapped her hands on her lap and sighed. "I just don't know what else I could tell you. I told you I don't really know John that well."

Weirdlee sat back in her chair and crossed her legs. "Well, let's start with the places he hangs out at. You mentioned before that he was a bar friend of yours. Did you go to many of the same bars he went to, or was it just one in particular?"

"One, basically. But I might run into him in other places, too. It's a small town."

"Sure. So was it O'Brien's that you both went to regularly?"

"Yeah. O'Brien's Pub."

"Still go there, do you?"

"Not really. I live in Florence now, so I don't go downtown too often anymore."

"I see," Weirdlee said with a nod. "And you weren't at O'Brien's on the night the Kerch girls disappeared, is that right?"

Saunders looked back at Weirdlee rather tensely, uncertain as to what she'd told her at their first meeting.

"I...don't think so," she said. "I don't remember being there."

Another nod from Weirdlee.

"What about Mr. Henneger's interests, Ms. Saunders," she continued. "Did he like to go fishing, or maybe camping—anything like that?"

Saunders laughed. "Fishing? Are you kidding me? No, that's not his thing."

Weirdlee smiled. "Not an outdoorsman, is he?"

"Not that I ever saw. He just worked and drank and worked and drank."

Weirdlee looked at her, surprised. "Wow. That's interesting. And how did that go over with Suzanne Kerch?"

Saunders shrugged and considered how to answer that. "I dunno. I guess it would have pissed her off, maybe. I wouldn't know."

The whole time Saunders and Weirdlee went back and forth, Saunders' heart kept pumping away.

Jesus Christ, she agonized to herself, *will you just let it fucking go!*

Weirdlee could sense the anxiety welling up inside of

Saunders. This was a woman with a dark secret she wasn't coming forth with. Why else would someone be so tense about answering a couple of mundane questions?

Weirdlee, of course, wasn't at all off the mark in how she felt. True enough, this was her maiden assignment in the field, but it wasn't her first experience in questioning people or evaluating evidence. She had a gifted sense about her—a peculiar kind of deductive reasoning that some might call second sight—that was one of the reasons Marvin Ledds had found her so...*useful*. There were other reasons, too—mysterious ones—that had led him to recruit her while she was still in her sophomore year at Brandeis, where she majored in health sciences. Prior to Ledds, people in high places at the university had noticed things about her, too, and they'd talked to each other about what they had seen. These people, in turn, talked to other people, until—soon enough—the government inevitably got involved. First came the CIA. Weirdlee, though, seemed a bit too odd and casual for their liking. Afterwards then, Assistant Director Ledds got word of her. He contacted her, and the two had several conversations. Unlike the stiff, business-like CIA, Ledds kept his chats with Weirdlee quite cordial. He had a much better appreciation of who—and more importantly, *what*—she truly was. The two became friendly to a degree that in just a short time, Ledds was able to coax her into testing for the Bureau. Everything worked out perfectly fine thereafter. Weirdlee worked for the FBI—and Ledds directly—while finishing school. She left Brandeis then as a four-year undergraduate and spent the next two years with the Bureau's International Operations Division in Washington D.C. Finally, then, after Ledds had learned about this case, he decided it was time to unleash his little prize upon the unsuspecting world.

And here she was.

"What about his vacations, Ms. Saunders?" Weirdlee asked. "Does Mr. Henneger go off on any trips—say, for a week or more?"

Saunders had no idea where this was leading to. "He might. I don't know. I don't think he ever talked about that, though."

"He'd go to the car races, though," Weirdlee suggested, the "r" in her "car" noticeably absent in her Boston drawl.

"Oh, yeah," Saunders recalled. "Yeah, he'll go up to New Hampshire, I guess. But not for a week or anything. Maybe a day or two?"

"You ever go with him?"

Saunders shook her head. "No. I never went with him. I never went anywhere with him."

Weirdlee examined Saunders quietly. The woman, in turn, noticed the agent's focus, and she glanced away uncomfortably, saying, "I think I should get back to work soon."

"Okay," Weirdlee said. "That's all I've got for now. We'll be in touch, Ms. Saunders."

As Weirdlee got up from her seat, Saunders appeared alarmed by what she'd said.

"For now?" she asked. "I thought you said you had just a couple more questions and we're done?"

Weirdlee pulled her purse over her shoulder. "When the investigation's over, Ms. Saunders, we'll be done."

Saunders rose from her chair. She didn't know what to say. She was trapped, it seemed. They were never going to let it go!

"Have a good night, Ms. Saunders."

Saunders snapped her eyes to Weirdlee as the agent walked away. "Good night," she said to her, her voice shaken.

Weirdlee left the room.

All at once, then, a sickening feeling overwhelmed Saunders, and she clutched her head in both her hands. Why—oh, why!—were they questioning her *now*—after all these years! They must have had *something* to go on, she agonized.

She put her hands together and interlocked her fingers, as if praying for some ray of hope.

There had to be something she could do!

Maybe, she told herself, they might let her out of this somehow. Maybe, if she told them everything she did and everything she knew, they might look past her own sins in this awful nightmare. She didn't actually kill those girls, after all. *No!* She didn't! If only she could tell them that and let them know how afraid she was. Afraid of going to prison. Afraid of Henneger. Afraid of—

The faces of Suzy and Becky Kerch flashed into her mind. Their deathly features, most horribly, appeared exactly as she'd last seen them ten years before, still frozen in their last contorted expressions of terror, their glassy dead eyes peering out from under half-closed eyelids, gazing directly at her.

Leave me alone! she cried out to them in silence, her mind tormented for so long by their memory!

My God, will you leave me alone!

12

A Spectre in the Dark

By 7:40 PM, O'Brien's Pub had peaked for its midweek crowd. The after-work patrons had been around for a couple of hours by then, and some of them were presently getting ready to call it a night.

Barry Funk was there, as usual, sitting at the end of the bar hunched over a draft beer. The Wednesday night bartender—an older, chubby guy wearing a food-stained white golf shirt and baggy cargo shorts—lazily patrolled the bar, appearing more interested in calling it a night himself than keeping his customers happy.

"Phil!" cried out John Henneger over the din of the masses. "I'm empty, man."

The bartender looked at him with a tired expression. "'Kay," he said with a nod.

Hearing him shout at the bartender, Funk looked over at Henneger. Through his drunken eyes, he saw the man still wore his dirty, mud-stained clothing, damp still from working outside in the pouring rain that day. At O'Brien's Pub, most people tended not to go home and change before coming out. They just showed up in whatever clothes they'd worked in that day.

"Shit..." Funk swore under his breath, grinning at him. He got up from his seat then and, beer in hand, sauntered over to the bar where Henneger sat.

"Yo," he said, clunking his beer down on the bar next to him. "You work all day in this shit, John?"

Henneger looked at him with weary eyes. Funk was just a punk—not someone you got all happy about when he came up to chat with you. "Most of the day," he said to him. "Fuck it."

Funk glanced about the place. "You seen Freddy in here tonight?"

Henneger looked around himself. "Nope."

"He was comin' outta the police station earlier today," Funk tattled, just as Fred had feared.

Henneger snapped his attention to Funk. "*What?*"

"Yeah." Funk chuckled. "He told me they picked him up for, uh, drunk in public or somethin'. You believe that shit?"

No. Henneger didn't.

The bartender arrived with his beer. Being a regular, Henneger had a tab going, so no money was exchanged.

"What time was this?" Henneger asked Funk.

"Oh, I dunno...maybe about two or three o'clock."

That weasely son of a bitch, Henneger fumed.

The FBI girl was getting to him, sure enough.

"Anyone with him?" he asked Funk.

"Nope. He was on his own. It was *pouring* out."

Henneger took down a long, thirsty swig of his fresh beer.

"But if I know him," Funk went on, "he's probably gettin' shit-faced at Benson's."

That, unfortunately, was an accurate assumption of Fred's life. Each and every day, he'd just get up in the morning and wait for the bars to open. Then he'd make the downtown rounds on foot. Sure enough, he would spend *hours* at each place—a dangerous habit for someone who might have somebody looking for him.

"Fuckin' guy..." Henneger muttered, his anger surging inside of him.

Just then, the front door opened and in walked a person

Henneger was quite surprised to see.

"John," Lisa Saunders called out—panic in her voice and in her eyes as she hurried over to him.

He snarled at her as she drew up close. "What are *you* doing here?"

She grabbed him by his arm. "I gotta talk to you, John."

He pulled his arm back. "What the fuck?" He got up then and grabbed a hold of her own arm. He led her off to the corner of the backside of the bar, away from prying ears. The latent music in the place helped mask their words, and he spoke to her in a hushed and angry voice.

"I told you not to come back here till things cooled down."

"Fuck, John," she shot back, fear in her eyes. "The FBI talked to me twice. They're fuckin' with me bad."

Henneger shook her briskly in his grasp. "You need to calm the fuck down. They ain't got nothin' unless you start talkin'."

She replied to him, pleading, "But I didn't do anything." Then she whispered more urgently, "I didn't kill those girls!"

Henneger swatted her cheek with an open hand. "Shut up!"

One of the patrons at the bar noticed Henneger's slap and spoke up. "Hey! What the fuck's going on over there?"

Henneger fired back at him, "Mind your own fuckin' business! I'll kick your ass!"

Saunders waved the guy off. "Don't fuck with him. It's all right."

The man hesitated, thinking things over, before turning back to the bar. A few other patrons looked on, too, but were out of earshot for any eavesdropping.

Henneger turned back to Saunders. He leered at her and jabbed a finger at her. "You're as guilty as I am, girl. You helped me carry them bitches around. Don't you tell me you didn't do nothin'." He glanced around, making sure they were well away from anyone else, before eyeing her again. "We get caught, you're going away for the rest of your life, just like me. Conspiracy, girl. You helped me dump 'em and then cover it up."

Saunders broke into tears. She mumbled, "But I didn't kill them, John. I didn't—"

Henneger jabbed a finger at her again. "You're going to fuckin' prison, you dumb bitch. They don't care if you killed 'em yourself or not. You helped me all the way, and you're going fuckin' down if you snitch on me."

Saunders pleaded, "I don't want to go to prison, John. I *can't*."

"Then you better shut your fuckin' mouth—and keep it shut. They got nothin' on us, you hear me? If they did, they woulda brought us both in. They got fuckin' *nothin'!*"

Saunders trembled as she eyed Henneger. She wanted to believe him. She wanted to believe that he knew what he was talking about, and that everything was going to be all right. Deep in the back of her mind, though, there was a darkness hidden away inside of her—a guilt-ridden cancer that she could never rid herself of. And it sickened her so! Those girls, she knew, were dead and gone, never to be seen alive on this earth again. They would never laugh. They would never love. No one would ever hold them in their arms and comfort them, and they would never have a chance to live a long and happy life. All of that was taken away from them, ten long years ago.

Tears streamed down her cheeks, and she whispered to Henneger, "I just want it all to go away."

Henneger glanced around again before saying to her in a more easy tone, "It ain't goin' away, Lisa. It's a secret we gotta keep till we're both dead and gone. We just gotta keep our mouths shut, and we're both good till the day we die. I'm telling you, girl." He wiped her tears from her cheeks. "Now you get yourself outta here. Go home before one of them agents comes by and sees you here."

Saunders looked off to the crowded bar. "They'll blab about it anyway."

Henneger eyed the crowd himself. "Maybe. That fuckin' Freddy's been yappin' too much, I know that."

"Freddy Duncan?" Saunders asked.

He looked at her. "Yeah. That dumb fuck. He's in love with that witch FBI chick. I'm gonna have to straighten his ass out for good."

"What do you mean?"

"I mean, I'm gonna shut that ole man's mouth once and for all. Fuck him."

Saunders shook her head. "I...I don't..."

Henneger smirked at her. "Don't worry. I ain't gonna ask you to help me carry him. You fuckin' cry baby."

"I don't wanna know nothin' about it," Saunders said in a panic.

"You ain't gonna know nothin'," Henneger snarled. "Just get your ass home and keep your mouth shut. If the Feds find out you were here, just tell 'em we were talking about some money you owe me. Eighty bucks sounds about right."

Saunders stared back at him. "Eighty..."

"Yeah," Henneger nodded. "Now take off."

Saunders swallowed hard, and she glanced around once more before hurrying out of the bar.

****

The night drew on, dark and dreary, as Joanna Weirdlee strolled into Maximilian's, a downtown tavern just up the road from O'Brien's Pub that specialized in serving up literally dozens of locally brewed beers. The atmosphere inside was warm and inviting, with a soft light and a rustic feel to it. Booths lined the right side of the place, while a long, antique wooden bar took up the left side. An array of beer taps filled up both the bar and the wall behind it. The food served at Maximilian's was quite good—better than most pubs—and presently the usual evening crowd of diners had filled most of the bar seats and all of the tables. Weirdlee, dressed still in her long gray raincoat to protect her from the damp, misty air outside, already had a spot in mind as she walked along the length of the bar.

"Is this seat taken?" she asked a man sitting at the bar, while pointing to a chair just to his right.

The man, she knew, was Hadley Police Sergeant Jim Banning, presently off duty and dressed in civilian clothes.

He glanced up at her. "No," he said. "Help yourself."

Weirdlee smiled at him, and she removed her raincoat, wrapping it over the seat's back, before taking a seat.

The bartender was quick to spot her, and came up to greet her.

"Can I help you?"

"A merlot," Weirdlee said. "Surprise me."

The bartender smiled. "Sure."

He stepped away.

Weirdlee looked at Banning, who had turned his attention back to his draft beer and dinner for the evening, a ham panini and french fries.

"I'm sort of new in town," she said to him, her Boston accent, as usual, evident in her speech. "I hope the wine is as popular as the beer appears to be."

Banning looked up and glanced about the bar, then looked at Weirdlee. "I couldn't tell you. I don't drink wine. Sorry."

He quickly went back to his meal.

The bartender brought over Weirdlee's wine. "Anything else?" he asked her, setting it down in front of her.

She shook her head. "No thank you."

He left her receipt at the edge of the bar and moved on.

Weirdlee picked up her glass of wine and gave it a sip. "Mmm," she hummed, "it's good."

She occasionally glanced at Banning while she sat there. He kept his attention on his dinner, though, seeming to be deep in his own thoughts and not interested in any company.

"You know," she said to him at length, "it's sort of been hit or miss for me visiting places since I got here. I suppose I should probably hire a tour guide." She finished with a coy smile.

Banning turned to her with a dull, serious expression of his own. "I'm a police officer, miss," he said to her. "I don't do tours."

Weirdlee raised an eyebrow, feigning surprise. "Well...really? Small world, isn't it? I'm with law enforcement, too."

That got his attention. He turned to face her directly. "Really?" he said. "Where at?"

Weirdlee put up a "one moment" finger. She fetched her purse from her oversized raincoat pocket, then pulled out her billfold and flashed her FBI identification.

Banning immediately rolled his eyes.

"Oh, Jesus," he sighed, "you're with them other guys."

"Other guys?" Weirdlee asked.

"The two heroes who showed up last weekend and accused us of not doing our job."

Again, Weirdlee feigned ignorance. "*No*. Did they, really? I'm sure it wasn't intentional. It couldn't have been."

Banning nodded. "Oh, it was intentional, all right." He gave Weirdlee a second look then as he picked up on her accent. "You from the Boston office, or something?"

"No," she replied. "I'm not from Boston."

"Well," Banning said, "I think your compatriots have worn out their welcome here, putting us all on wild goose chases."

Weirdlee nodded, and then took another sip of her wine.

"I suppose it's annoying," she said then, "having to do the same things all over again when you already know what the outcome will be."

Banning drank from his beer, then muttered, "Damn right," under his breath.

"Still," Weirdlee added, "there's a purpose to everything in life, they say."

Banning put down his beer and looked at Weirdlee again. "What about you?" he asked. "What do you think about all this searching and re-searching going on?"

Weirdlee allowed her pleasant demeanor to fade. "Right off," she said, "I can think of two women who'd appreciate us not giving up on them, if they could do such a thing. I know for sure of one woman who does."

Banning guessed which woman she meant. "You mean Mrs. Whiting? The sister?"

Weirdlee gave a nod.

"Yeah, well, she thinks we fucked it all up, too," he said. He picked up a portion of his panini and held it in both hands for a moment. He stewed quietly, doubt swirling in his mind, before abruptly slapping the sandwich back onto his plate. "Hell," he fumed, "maybe she's right, after all. Maybe we just fucked everything up back then."

"You don't mean that," Weirdlee said.

He looked at her. "Yeah, I do. And I'm sick and tired of telling everyone they got it all wrong. Maybe we did fuck it up."

"But you followed procedure," said Weirdlee. "You did

everything you were supposed to do."

Banning eyed her, his emotions—and his beer—getting the better of him. "Yeah, well, maybe the 'procedure' was fucked up, then. Maybe we should have said 'Fuck it' and went after that guy quicker."

"You're second guessing yourself."

"I'm not," Banning insisted. "I'm just being honest with myself. What else can I do?"

"You did your job back then, Sergeant," said Weirdlee, letting slip that she knew his rank—and so who he was—all along.

Banning stared at her. He'd caught the "Sergeant" reference, but there was something else about the woman, too. Was she patronizing him?

"What do you want from me, lady?" he asked her.

Weirdlee took another sip of her wine. Then she set her glass down and said to him, "I'd like you to help us solve a crime, officer. To right a wrong that was committed ten years ago, in a little town that doesn't deserve to have such a heavy burden put upon the people who live and work there."

Banning turned himself back to the bar. He took up his beer in his hands, and he eyed it for a moment in silence. Then he asked Weirdlee, his voice tinged with emotion, "You know what I honestly hope happens?"

Weirdlee pursed her lips, and she kept an easy smile as she answered him. "That my partners and I should fall flat on our faces?" she guessed, even knowing it wasn't true.

"*No...*" Banning replied in anguish. "I would never hope for something like that." He turned to face Weirdlee directly, and he spoke to her in a pained voice. "I hope you guys do what we couldn't do. I hope you find those girls, and I hope that son of a bitch, Henneger, goes down. I only wish to God I could have been the one to put the cuffs on him. I swear, seeing him walk around free all these years is killing me inside. It's *killing me*." He took a swig of his beer, swallowing it hard. "I lie awake at night, you know, and I just can't get him out of my head. And I see those girls, their faces, and I don't know how much longer I can take it anymore." He wiped his watery eyes. "I hope to God you find out what happened to them. I truly do hope for that, more than anything else. I swear to God I do." He took another chug of his beer.

Weirdlee gazed at the heart-stricken police officer. She knew, in her soul, that his pain was genuine, and that he had been suffering on his own for far too long.

Just like Sandy Whiting, he deserved to see some measure of justice to come into his life.

"We'll do our best," she whispered to him.

Banning took in a breath, and he glanced around while recovering his emotions. He looked at Weirdlee's wine glass then, which lay almost empty. "You like another glass of wine?" he asked her, his voice still weak. "I'm buying."

Weirdlee smiled warmly, but she shook her head just the same. "No thank you," she said. "One's enough for me. I've got some work to do, still."

Banning gave her a nod, returning her smile. He found himself, quite surprisingly, very much at ease in her company. And though he truly wished the pretty agent would stay with him for just a little while longer, he also knew, just as well, that she and her partners hadn't come to town for such pleasantries.

"Fair enough," he said to her. "Thanks for talking with me tonight."

****

Fred Duncan stepped gingerly down the front steps of

Benson's, arriving safely on the sidewalk along Masonic Street. First glancing to his left and right to check for traffic, he crossed the street then, his head tilted upward to the cloudy evening sky. The steady rain of the day had let up to a light mist by this time, and Fred found the cool spray peppering his face delightfully refreshing. It was just after 9:30 PM on this July evening, and, while not usually pitch-dark at this time of year, the thick cloud cover had imposed a more thorough darkness than would otherwise be the case at that hour.

Fred walked a short distance up the sidewalk until he arrived at a public parking lot, which he then entered. This particular lot took up a good portion of the backside of several buildings that fronted the city's Main Street, off to his right. The lot itself, along with a couple of other smaller lots that adjoined it at its far and rear sides, was set much lower than Main Street, so that anyone coming in from that street would be driving—or walking—down slope to get to the lots. Fred most often would use these lots as shortcuts to get to his next stops during the course of his drinking nights, though on this night he presently had only his bed as an intended destination.

Chain link fences partitioned each of the parking lots. Each fence also had a small opening at some point along its length to allow for pedestrian walk-throughs. Also, at the right end of the lot that Fred currently traversed, an alleyway led directly up to Main Street—although Fred wasn't heading that way on this night. Instead, he made for the fence opening that led into the far-side adjoining lot.

Having made this trip many times before, Fred usually walked along without paying much attention to his immediate surroundings. Tonight being no different, his thoughts drifted ahead to the upcoming weekend and his planned bus trip up to Greenfield to see his daughter. He pictured her face in his mind, and he smiled. Kelly was much too good for him, really. He always felt out of place in her company. He would go up there to visit with her, but only for a couple of hours each time. Then he'd hurry back to Northampton, eager to get back to O'Brien's Pub or Benson's, or wherever else his friends might be that day, and settle in for yet another afternoon drunk. He enjoyed it, really. It's all he had in his life. And Kelly always seemed to understand, too, which made everything all right. She'd see him staring off as she tended to things or chatted with him, and she'd say to him, "Bored, dad?" And he'd say back to her, "Yeah, a little." Then she'd let him be on his way pretty soon afterward.

An unexpected chill came over Fred as he staggered drunkenly along. *Damn it*, he swore to himself. He'd forgotten his umbrella at the bar.

Oh well. Pick it up tomorrow.

As he continued on, his foggy, injured mind drifted off to what he'd been through the past couple of days.

The FBI girl! She was so pretty! And he remembered their last conversation—it had frightened him so! But she'd been very nice to him, still, and so unlike all the others he knew who teased him about his slow-mindedness. He recalled, as well, what she had said to him as they sat there in The Corner Bistro: "We're the good guys, you and I."

He thought about Suzanne and Rebecca Kerch then. Those poor girls. He wondered what might have become of them if they'd lived beyond that terrible day. He wondered if the daughter, Becky, might have been anything like his own daughter. And then, quite suddenly, a deep sadness touched his heart as he imagined how he'd feel if someone took away his beloved Kelly.

No!

He ached inside, heartbroken at the mere thought of it

all.

I'll help you, he promised Weirdlee.

I'm one of the good guys.

Off in the darkness of the wet and dreary night, Fred thought he heard footsteps coming up behind him. He stopped and turned around.

Squinting, he peered into the shadows. "Who's there?" he asked into the blackened, faceless night.

No answer.

He turned back around and started off once more.

The footsteps, however, quickly returned.

Or was it merely raindrops?

He looked up at the sky to see, and perhaps to feel upon his face, if it was raining again.

Nope.

"Hey, old man," said someone from off behind him.

Freddy knew the voice anywhere. It was John Henneger. He snapped his eyes to him, there to see his dark shape approaching.

"John?" he asked. "Whaddya doing out here?"

Henneger stepped out of the shadows to reveal himself, a phony grin planted on his face.

"Just headin' to Benson's, my man. Where you off to?"

Fred shrugged. "Oh, I was just goin' home. I'm bushed."

Henneger came up closer to Fred's side. He kept both of his hands down, and his right hand cupped. In that hand, he secured his trusty butterfly knife—a handy tool for intimidating anyone who decided to fuck with him. Or for tending to things in a more deadly fashion, if the need ever arose.

"It's dangerous out here, Freddy. The summer brings out the baddies, you know."

Fred laughed at that. "Yeah, right." Then he glanced around at the darkness surrounding them, where only a dim ray of light from the nearby alleyway leading up to Main Street peeked through. "Think I'll be okay."

"Come on," Henneger said, nodding in a direction that led farther into the shadows. "I'll go along with ya till we get up to Center, then you can go on from there."

"You ain't gotta do that," Fred said.

Henneger lost his smile. He grabbed hold of Fred's shoulder with his free hand and shoved him ahead. "Fuck I don't!" he said roughly. "You talk too much, asshole!"

Fred's heart leapt to his throat. "W-what?"

"Fuck with your friends, boy, you lose 'em," Henneger growled, stalking up to him. "Fuckin' asshole."

Fred's throat tightened. He could barely speak.

"I..." he quaked, "I...I..."

He was about to be killed.

Henneger made his move.

"Fred," came a woman's voice then, firm and clear, from off by the alleyway.

Henneger stopped.

Fred turned, there to see none other than Joanna Weirdlee, her slim shape silhouetted by the dim glow of the streetlights up on Main Street behind her. He nearly fell apart in relief at the sight of her.

"Come here," she said to him.

Henneger turned to her himself. He eyed her black shape set against the glow of the lights.

"Just walkin' the man home, lady," he said to her with a smarmy grin.

She ignored him.

"Come with me, Fred," she said in an unwavering tone. "I'll take you home."

Fred stared at her, his heart racing. With his poor eyesight, he could only see a blurry rendering of her. Even so, she was beautiful! And her voice—or at least the muted tones he could hear of it—was like an angel's, soft and sweet and gentle in its tone.

He glanced back at Henneger, and then to Weirdlee again. What should he do?

"Fred..." Weirdlee said, not giving up on him. "Come with me, now."

Henneger stared at her. Unlike what Fred saw and heard from her, though, the woman he saw was wicked in her presence, with a cold, edgy voice that gave evidence to her authority amongst them, both real and surreal.

He pulled his captive gaze away from her and turned to Fred.

"I'll walk you home, man," he said. "Fuck the FBI."

Fred remained hesitant, though. He took a step back from Henneger. "I-I dunno."

Weirdlee stepped forward then, her shoes clacking against the parking lot's wet pavement. "Come along, now," she said to Fred. "It's time for you to go home."

Henneger cast a leering eye to her. Her black, silhouetted form, he saw, soaked up the shadows all around her. Her eyes, like blood-red coals, shone in the night air.

She was a witch, all right. And she wasn't going away.

He slid his butterfly knife into his pants pocket. *No sense in getting carried away,* he figured. Besides, she was probably packing a pistol, too. And what was that old saying? Never bring a knife to a gunfight?

"Don't matter to me," he said to her aloud. He stepped away from Fred.

Fred scooted off then to join Weirdlee, and she smiled at him as he came up to her. "Let's get you home," she said to him, her angelic voice so endearing to his heart!

He replied eagerly, "Okay!"

The two of them started up the alleyway together, heading back up to Main Street.

Giddy in her company, Fred confessed to his protector, "I was really afraid back there."

"Fred," she said to him, "why didn't you call me after you went to the police station? I gave you my card."

Fred stared back at her. *Her business card.*

"I...I forgot all about it."

Weirdlee shook her head and chided him playfully, "What am I going to do with you?"

"I'm sorry," he gushed.

Arriving on Main Street, Weirdlee locked an arm around Fred's, escorting him as they walked.

"It's okay," she said to him. "Let's get you home, now."

Back in the parking lot, meanwhile, Henneger watched them leave.

Catch you later, Freddy, he said to himself. The retribution he sought, in his mind, had only been delayed.

He settled his glare on Weirdlee, then, just as she slipped beyond his sight.

Gonna get me some of you, too, he vowed.

One way or another.

13

Coming to Terms

Located on the property of a former horse racing track, the Fort River Birding and Nature Trail was a still-under-construction preserve bordering the south bank of the small, serpentine Fort River. A crew of volunteers, mostly teenagers, had been building a pathway that included elevated walkways and observation decks that roughly circumnavigated the former track area. On this Thursday morning, the place was deserted save for a few Hadley PD officers and the Guardian GPR team assigned to them for the day's search.

Hadley Police Chief Towers stood by the edge of the preserve, there along with Sergeant Banning as the two watched the GPR team set up their equipment. The search would be undertaken all along the wriggling river's southern and northern banks, as well as in the river itself. For the latter job, three more officers had put on waders, and presently they stood nearby the southern bank of the river.

"We'll give this about a half day's work, anyway," said a disinterested Towers to Banning.

Banning, his hands on his hips and his eyes hidden under dark sunglasses as he eyed the GPR team, replied to the chief, "He mighta dumped the bodies here, Chief, and then they could have been carried off downstream. It's been a few years."

Towers eyed his subordinate with an annoyed

expression. "Well, what do you want us to do? Search the whole goddamned river?"

Banning shrugged and pointed off to the western edge of the preserve, where the little Fort River snaked its way downstream until it eventually fed into the larger Connecticut River. "We could at least follow the river, here, down to the Connecticut, sir. It ain't that far."

"Shit," Towers swore. "I don't have the manpower nor the time to search all the way back to the Connecticut River, Jim. What the hell's gotten into you, man?"

Banning shook his head, then turned to his boss.

"I don't know..." he said ruefully, "I've just been thinking, that maybe if we did things a little more thoroughly the first time around, we might not be doing this today."

Towers leered at him. "Who the hell have you been talking to? What are you talking about?"

"I just think, Chief, maybe we should have searched Henneger's house the day the woman's boss called. You know? Right then and there."

Towers shook his head. "No," he said firmly. "We're not gonna do this, Sergeant. We're not gonna start second-guessing ourselves and blaming each other for something that happened a long time ago. We went right by the book on this one."

Banning looked off and muttered, "Fuck the book..."

"Sergeant," Towers barked. "Knock it off. You hear me? You're letting the FBI get the better of you. You're starting to doubt yourself."

Banning's temper flared. He turned to Towers. "I've been doubting myself for ten years, Chief. *Ten fucking years!*"

Towers gave him a swat on the arm and scolded him in a hushed voice. "Shut up, Jim. What the fuck is the matter with you?"

Banning looked around, suddenly aware that he was making a scene. He turned back to Towers and said to him in a lowered voice, "I just want to get that bastard, Chief, and I don't care if it's our guys that get him or the FBI. I just want him in prison or in his grave."

Towers stared back at Banning, taken aback by his subordinate's sudden show of frustration.

"Well, shit," he said to him, "we all want that, Jim. We all want to see that asshole put away."

Banning pleaded to his superior, "Let's go to the river, then, Chief. All the way. No 'good enoughs' this time around. 'Cause I don't want to lie awake at night wondering what we might have found if we'd gone just a little farther along."

Towers kept his eyes on Banning as he considered how to respond to him. It would be a long day, indeed, if "good enough" meant searching the Fort River all the way to the Connecticut River.

"Okay," he finally said to him then. "All the way to the river, it is."

****

Morning at the Hotel Northampton saw Special Agents Nicks, Fielding, and Weirdlee rendezvous at the Coolidge Park Cafe for a light breakfast and a catch-up chat. The two men had eggs and toast with coffee while Weirdlee opted for a cup of yogurt and hot tea. The agents sat out on the cafe's patio overlooking King Street.

"Anything new and interesting from our interviews, so far?" Nicks asked his colleagues.

Fielding waved a dismissive hand. "Nobody knows anything, man. It's like askin' if they remember cuttin' their own lawns ten years ago. And Henneger ain't done nothin' to lose any friends in the past ten years, either. So that ain't helpin'."

"Yeah," Nicks agreed. "Locals tend to stick together, that's for sure."

Weirdlee licked some yogurt from her spoon. "I managed to find one man willing to help, anyway."

Nicks jabbed a finger at her, remembering their previous conversation. "That's right. Did that guy ever make it to the police station?"

She replied with a nod, "He did," and then set down her yogurt. "He's in trouble for it, too."

Nicks sat up in his seat. "He is? What do you mean?"

"Henneger found out somehow," Weirdlee explained. "He had him in a back alley last night. Alone and up to no good."

"He wouldn't dare do anything to that guy," said Fielding. "Not with us around."

Weirdlee tilted her head, musing. "Actually, I think he intended to kill Mr. Duncan."

"Noo..." Fielding replied. "That would be crazy."

"And a little obvious," added Nicks. "More than likely, he might have wanted to intimidate him. Scare him."

Weirdlee looked at Nicks with an emotionless stare. "He meant to kill him, Sam."

"Were you there?" Fielding asked her.

She turned to him. "I was. Just in time, too, I think."

Nicks leaned forward in his chair, eyeing Weirdlee. "What time was this?"

"Oh..." Weirdlee recalled, "about ten o'clock or so. Maybe earlier."

Nicks was none too pleased with that. "You went into a back alley and confronted Henneger at ten o'clock at night?"

"I did."

"I hope you were packin'," Fielding cut in.

She looked to him. "Of course."

"Still," said Nicks. "Not a wise decision. He could have had friends back there—Henneger, I mean."

"It was only him and Mr. Duncan."

"Wasn't it dark out?" asked Fielding.

She nodded. "Oh, yes."

"Then how did you know?"

She smiled wryly at him. "I just had a good sense of things, is all." She raised an eyebrow. "Call it...woman's intuition?"

Fielding drummed his lips, eying her. "Call it lucky, more likely."

"Next time, call us up," Nicks advised Weirdlee. "Even if we can't get there right away, we'll at least know where you are."

She smiled at him. "Sure."

Fielding asked her then, "So what'd he have to say, anyway? That Duncan fella."

Nicks answered, having already been briefed by Weirdlee the day before. "He's got Henneger leaving the bar a lot earlier than when Henneger said he left. And that means maybe he was home when the girls disappeared— *before* they disappeared."

"Oh yeah?" Fielding said, eying Nicks.

Weirdlee added, "And that means he lied in his police report."

Fielding remained skeptical, though. "But that don't mean he killed 'em. There still ain't no evidence."

"It's a hole, though," Nicks said. "And maybe if we can get that Saunders woman to talk to us some more, we might punch a few more holes in his story."

"I think she's about ready to cave," said Weirdlee. "If we

can approach her with some evidence, then she might be open to some kind of deal."

Nicks frowned at that. "Unfortunately, we're not likely to find any more evidence until someone starts talking to us. Me and Agent Fielding, here, have gone through all the crime scene files. There's nothing there to re-examine."

"You want me to talk to her again, anyway?" Weirdlee asked.

"No," Nicks replied. "Let's wait till all our searches are done for the day. Then maybe you can ask her about her whereabouts on the night the girls disappeared—being sure to mention that we know Henneger left earlier that night than when he told us, of course."

Weirdlee raised an eyebrow. "Of course."

Nicks finished, "Beyond that, it looks like, for now, we've got about as much info as we're going to get from the locals. Not exactly what I was hoping for, but there it is."

"We got much more places to search again after today?" Fielding asked.

Nicks leaned back in his seat and heaved a sigh. "We're about ready to wrap things up on the old searches, looks like. Chief Towers has his guys out in the sticks today, and the staties are finishing up with the Hop Brook search."

"Is that all we have?" Weirdlee asked him. "Old and new searches?"

Nicks gave her a nod. "Without any other info, we're just making guesses, really. I've got a list of places following along the route up to New Hampshire that Henneger *might* have stopped by. We can have the local cops in those areas check 'em out."

"What about new places around here?" asked Fielding.

Nicks pursed his lips, considering. "I've had the staties checking out a couple of spots, already. And the Northampton PD's been good about checking places, too."

Weirdlee sighed as she eyed her tea thoughtfully.

"He could have gone anywhere," she said in a tired voice. "This whole area is woods and swamps."

Fielding asked her, "So, what's your woman's intuition tell ya?"

She looked back at him morosely, and she answered, "I can't see that far."

Fielding gulped. His old friend had gotten back to him earlier that morning with some rather interesting information that made Weirdlee's history all the more intriguing—and her response to him just then all the more telling.

"Well," Nicks said, "we're just going to have to let it ride. See how things play out." He picked up his coffee to finish it. "How's our colleagues from Boston doing, Agent Fielding?"

Fielding got back to finishing his own breakfast as he answered. "Agent McDonald is over at his post in the motel parking lot, watching Mrs. Whiting. A state cop watched her overnight. Agent Seavers called me about an hour ago. He said that he followed Lisa Saunders to her job at the hospital. He's out having breakfast himself now."

"Okay," said Nicks. He took a moment to consider things, and then said, "I guess I'll swing by a couple of the search teams and see how things are going. I've got some phone calls to make, too, about those spots I mentioned going up to New Hampshire."

"You have just one route in mind, or a couple of 'em?" Fielding asked.

"A couple," Nicks replied.

Weirdlee finished up her tea and got up from her seat. "I guess I can go back to the courthouse and re-read all the police reports—again. Maybe something will come to me."

"Alrighty," said Nicks. He got up himself. "See you all

later, then."

****

It was late morning and Sandy Whiting lay on her motel bed, still dressed in her nightgown while watching a marathon of *CSI: Crime Scene Investigation* on the room's widescreen television set. Her mind drifted from one lingering daydream to another as scenes from the show passed by, half-unnoticed by her, to the point where she had no idea where the characters were in any given episode.

The shows, it occurred to her, were always so predictable. Some serious crime would be perpetrated, and the investigators would spring into action. Then—no matter how clever or devious the villain was—the stars of the show would invariably get their man. Or woman. That's the way it almost always went down. The good guys, naturally, always won in the end.

But that's not how things went in real life, Sandy knew all too well. Sometimes, the bad guys got away with murder. Sometimes, they lived out their whole lives never paying for the evil they'd done to others.

And she knew, lying there, that in her case things were not likely to go the way she'd hoped for, after all. Her husband, bless his soul, had been right all along. This was just a procedural check—a review, as it were, just to make sure they'd done everything right the first time around. There was no new evidence. No new witnesses had come forward. And, after all the searches were done and then a few others conducted thereafter, the FBI agents would be on their way, back to Washington or New York or wherever the hell else they'd come from. And she would go home, too, just as she had the first time, ten long years ago, sad and empty, her heart wrenched from her soul once more.

Justice, for Sandy Whiting, was just a word etched on a building. There were no heroes in the real world, anymore.

A knock on the door brought Sandy out of her brooding daydream.

"Yes?" she called out.

"Room service," came a muffled male voice from the other side of the door.

She gave the door a curious look. "I didn't order anything."

"A Mr. Richard Whiting called in. He ordered some green eggs and ham?"

Sandy smiled, and felt immediately at ease. The voice, after all, was her husband's. She shot up from her bed and pranced eagerly to the door. She unlocked it, swung it open, and there he was.

"Hey, stranger," he said to her, a bright smile lighting up his face.

She leapt into his arms, and he held her tightly as she hugged and kissed him repeatedly.

"Hey-hey, there," he said happily, "you miss me, or what?"

"I did," she said sincerely, looking into his eyes. Her warm smile was a welcome sight for him, too.

"Hey, so what's with the guy outside?" he asked her. "I had to show my ID to get in here."

She glanced out behind him, seeing the FBI agent, McDonald, standing there leaning against his car with his arms crossed. "Oh," she said, "they're just worried about me raising hell out here, so they got someone keeping tabs on me, I'm sure."

Richard laughed at that. "Yeah, I'm sure that's it."

Sandy gave her husband a curious look. "So, I thought you were mad at me, mister?"

He put his hands on her shoulders. "I was, at first. But I

couldn't stay that way. I know how you feel, hon, and I know how important this is to you."

She smiled back at him, though it faded quickly as her sadness returned. "Yeah. It was. You were right, though, Richard. There's nothing for me here. It's all just a rerun of everything they did before. Somebody's rechecking the paperwork, is all."

Richard looked at her thoughtfully. "Do you want to go home, then?"

She mulled the idea for a moment. Her heart tugged, though, at wanting to stay.

"Tomorrow, maybe," she offered. "I'll try to be home for dinner, anyway."

"Well," Richard said with a mischievous grin, "maybe we can just follow each other home, then, and I'll stick around here with you."

"Oh yeah?"

"Sure. You're not the only one with vacation time, you know. I called in today, and tomorrow's Friday. Who goes back to work on Fridays?"

Sandy tossed her arms around her man and hugged him tightly. "Oh, I love you, babe. Thank you so much."

"Okay then," he said, chuckling. "Love you, too."

Sandy drew herself back and smiled at Richard, glowingly and at ease. She wasn't alone anymore, and the dark and desperate thoughts that had so clouded her mind earlier had left her, at least for a little while.

She closed the door behind them.

****

Thursday afternoons in downtown Northampton were every bit as bustling as any other working day in the artsy little city. Storefronts and restaurants lined the main streets on both sides, and people packed the sidewalks as they went about their business. The city had a liberal flair to it, and the niche lifestyles of a diverse community were evident all around.

Special Agent Nicks strolled about the streets that early afternoon, the investigation weighing on his mind. Despite his focus, he still took the time, though, to admire the innocent, happy scenes that passed him by. Even the panhandlers looked happy to be there, plying their thankless trades, he noticed. They'd play their instruments or shine your shoes or merrily sing a tune. Anything, it seemed, to fetch a little reward for their efforts.

After wandering aimlessly for a time, Nicks found a place to hold up next to a newspaper stand. There, he stood watching and admiring the performance of a young violinist on the sidewalk as she played her instrument with the skill of a practiced pro. She was, he surmised, possibly a student, this being a college town. Perhaps on summer break and out to earn some extra cash to live on, in much the same way the older panhandlers did. The piece she performed was sweet and charming. The violin's strings sang along with the light breeze that cooled the warm summer air. The music set Nicks' mind at ease. There was something so very peaceful and so very comforting about the innocence of youth, just starting out in their lives. So much laughter and joy. So many stories not yet written or told. Everyone should grow up with a little innocence in their lives, Nicks mused. It was something even he enjoyed, not so very long ago.

"Nicks!" called out Special Agent Fielding, trotting up the sidewalk.

Distracted, Nicks snapped his eyes to his partner.

Fielding came up to him.

"Just got word from the Hadley boys," he said. "They're

searchin' the Fort River all the way to the Connecticut."

"Oh, yeah?" Nicks replied. "Good to hear."

"Yeah," Fielding said with a chuckle. "I wonder what's gotten into them boys. First we can't get 'em movin', now they're goin' out of their way."

"Good for them," Nicks said. "Though I'm not sure what good it'll do."

Fielding glanced around. He spotted the young woman playing the violin, then looked back at Nicks. "What are ya up to, here, partner?"

Nicks managed a pensive smile. "Oh...just enjoying the entertainment for a little bit."

Fielding looked again to the violinist. Talented as she was, her music wasn't exactly his cup of tea.

"I never got into the classical stuff, myself."

Nicks raised an eyebrow to that. He supposed, then, that anyone playing an instrument other than a guitar or banjo would probably be off the list of favorites for the southern-raised Fielding.

"Anything else for me?" he asked him then.

Fielding put his hands on his hips, considering things. "Uh, nope." Then, snapping his fingers, he suddenly remembered something he wanted to bring up. "Oh—uh, I did want to mention somethin' to ya, partner. It's about Special Agent Weirdlee."

"Agent Weirdlee?"

"Yeah."

"What about her?"

"Well..." Fielding began uneasily, "you know how she's been somewhat of a mystery girl to the both of us?"

Nicks shrugged. "I guess so."

"Yeah, well, I called in a favor from an old buddy of mine back in the Cyber Division. Had him do some snoopin' around for me."

Nicks glared at him. "You didn't."

Fielding nodded. "I did."

"Not very friendly of you, my man," Nicks said, shaking his head.

"Oh yeah? Well, not very friendly of her for not lettin' anyone know about her history and such."

"Does she know about *your* history?" asked Nicks.

"She would if she asked. Or just looked it up."

"I bet," said Nicks. "That still doesn't give you the right to pry into someone else's past. Especially a colleague."

"Hey—fair enough. But I had a bug in me, you know?"

Nicks folded his arms and pinched his bottom lip with his finger and thumb. "Does she know about your checking up on her?"

"Nope."

"You know she will, eventually."

"Probably," Fielding said with a shrug. Then he leered at his partner. "You wanna know what I found out, or are ya just gonna stand there judgin' me?"

Nicks smiled at that. "Go ahead. What's the big news?"

Fielding glanced around first, as if to make sure Weirdlee herself wasn't coming up on them.

"My buddy got back to me this morning," he began. "He found out that 'Weirdlee' is not our girlfriend's real last name."

Nicks raised an eyebrow. "It's not, huh?"

"Nope. She changed her name in her freshman year at Brandeis. You wanna know what it was before that?"

"Why not? Since you got it, anyway."

Fielding leaned in closer to Nicks. He said to him, slowly and hushed, "Osborne."

Nicks stared back at Fielding. He imagined the name was supposed to mean something special, but he couldn't figure out what that would be. "Ssso...?" he replied, expecting more.

Fielding grinned. "She ain't from Boston, either. But she's awfully close."

"Ahh," Nicks said with a nod. "So where is she from, then? And why do we care?"

"You ready for this?" Fielding said eagerly. He finished by pronouncing both of his forthcoming words slowly and deliberately.

"Salem, Massachusetts."

Nicks again stared blankly at him. "Salem," he repeated.

"Yeah," Fielding said, nodding. "Can you believe that?"

Nicks looked off at the passersby. The drama, for him, just wasn't there.

"So..." he said, "I guess her accent is for real."

"Osborne," Fielding continued, "was the name of one of them girls that was accused of being a witch during those witch trials they had back a-ways."

Nicks turned and eyed Fielding with a serious expression, beginning to see what he was suggesting. "The Salem witch trials," he clarified, "from a few hundred years ago?"

Fielding nodded. "Yeah. Ain't that somethin'? And my buddy dug a little deeper, too, 'cause he was so curious, himself. He found out...our Miss Weirdlee is a direct descendent of the girl in the trials. The girl's name was Sarah Osborne."

Nicks gave Fielding a thoughtful nod.

Truthfully, at that particular moment, he wasn't all that much interested in Weirdlee's lineage. The Kerch case still lingered heavily on his mind. He'd obsessed over all of the possible clues and evidence, all the impossible number of places they'd have to search or theorize about.

He looked off once more to the violinist, who still serenaded passersby. He watched then as a finely dressed man stopped before the woman, complimented her, and dropped a dollar into her open violin case that lay at her feet. She smiled, said thanks, and the man went on his way.

"You hear what I'm saying, Agent Nicks?"

Nicks looked back at Fielding. "Is Agent Weirdlee still at the courthouse?"

Fielding cast a puzzled expression, replying, "Huh? I dunno. Doubt it. She'da been there all morning."

"Get a hold of her. See if she is."

"What's this about?" Fielding asked.

"I want to pull a search warrant for Henneger's house."

Fielding glanced behind them, toward the distant Connecticut River and the town of Hadley, beyond. "His old one, or...?"

"His new one—here in Northampton."

"I, uh..."

"Look," Nicks explained, "if no one wants to talk to us, then fuck 'em. But we've been searching blind, here. We need to get into his house and look for any photos or souvenirs—things like that—that he may have picked up while out partying or on vacation. We need something to help guide us on where to go."

"The judge might ask us what—"

"He lied in his police report," Nicks shot back. "That's enough."

Fielding nodded. "Okay, partner. I'll head out there myself."

"Thanks."

Fielding turned and walked off smartly then.

Nicks ran a few more things through in his mind. Everyone has a favorite spot they go to, he figured, and everyone has a favorite route to get there by. It was a long shot, for sure. But then, this whole investigation—since the first day they got there—was one big pie-in-the-sky long shot.

His attention found its way back to the young violinist. Her music, for him, was like food for the soul.

He walked over to where she stood, and he smiled at her as she played on. She saw him there and returned his smile. He dug into his back pocket then and pulled out his wallet. Opening it, he slid a twenty-dollar bill from its fold.

"Thanks," he said to her sincerely, and he dropped the bill into her open case.

She beamed back at him. "Thank *you*, sir!"

Nicks smiled and gave her a parting nod. Then he walked off to get on with things.

****

Calvin Coolidge is most widely known these days as the 30th President of the United States of America. Less well known is that he was also a governor of Massachusetts, a state legislator there, and, even more locally, a former mayor of a little city named Northampton.

His fame—both national and local—was why the cafe at the Hotel Northampton bore his name, and why the bridge spanning the Connecticut River along Route 9 was likewise named in his honor.

Tucked nearby this bridge, on its northwest side, was a small riverside park where joggers, bicyclists, and leisurely strollers often visited. This was also where another bridge— a former railroad bridge located just north of the park— spanned the river. This bridge had long ago been remade into a pedestrian bridge, and it was from here that most walkers and bicyclists traversed the Connecticut.

Special Agent Weirdlee presently strolled along the pedestrian bridge, her thoughts drifting from past to present in a collage of memories and daydreams. Dressed in her trademark dark pantsuit and wearing her sunglasses, she clutched a half-finished bottle of Dr. Pepper in her hand, which she nursed from time to time as she walked along.

She took in the pleasant scenery all around her while making her way back towards the Northampton side of the river. Soon arriving at the bridge's western side, she took a left from there and then followed a dirt path leading to the little riverside park. Once there, she strolled along another path that snaked its way down to a lower part of the park, and which then led her to a set of rudimentary docks floating on the Connecticut River itself.

The day was warm and beautiful, and the cloudless sky reflected its blue hue amongst the little waves that sparkled in the sunshine. Weirdlee took in the river, her eyes wandering about its expanse as it meandered southward. Deciding then to rest for a bit, she settled herself onto the dock, sitting cross-legged at the edge of it, looking south.

Her mind weighed heavily on the case at hand. Things, so far, had not been going the way she'd imagined they'd go. True, this was her first field assignment. But even so, she expected more progress than this. She thought her abilities—the reason Assistant Director Ledds had brought her out there in the first place—would have been of greater benefit to the team. Instead, they were at a dead end, it seemed, and no closer to cornering that murderous Henneger than when they'd started the investigation that previous weekend.

Why, she asked herself, could she not see what was happening more clearly? Her second sight—that inherent ability that Ledds had found so priceless in her—wasn't showing her the way, as she'd been so certain it would. There were no faces in her mind from which to divine a sure direction. Instead, she heard only voices, or distant echoes of a sort, barely discernible in her head.

She sipped her Dr. Pepper while sitting there. Then she set the bottle down beside her and sighed wearily, looking off again to the slow moving river, whose ripples entranced her, casting thoughts and memories through her mind. She focused on the watery reflections of sky and nature all around her, so calming and serene they were, while searching for a sign to help guide her on her way.

When she was a child growing up in Salem, it was common knowledge that Joanna was not at all like the other little girls she played with. In school, the shy young lady found very few friends, and even those drifted away from her once her high school years began. Oftentimes, she'd be teased and mocked by her classmates for being so different from everyone else. For being so...*weird*.

Her parents tried to convince her that her so-called "special abilities" were just a figment of her vivid imagination. *Stop it*, they'd tell her. Everyone has déjà vu, they said. Everyone thinks they can tell things about people—see things. That doesn't mean we have magical powers. Not you, Joanna Osborne. Not you.

So, as time passed, young Joanna sheltered herself in her mind, closing off everyone from her gifted but lonely soul. She never dated or socialized with anyone. She never had those intimate talks with a lover or a friend. It was just her. Always and forever, it seemed. Only just her.

The whole time, too, she immersed herself in the intricacies of the Craft. She was never truly Wiccan in her beliefs—that being the spiritual part of the lifestyle that so many others gravitated to. It was the magick, only, that drew her in. The powers of second sight and witchcraft—she had them both, it seemed. Except for that she was all alone with these marvelous gifts in an otherwise mundane, uninspiring world.

Until, that is, Ledds came along. That pudgy, charming old man. He told her things that she had never heard before. Like how smart she was, and how pretty she was, and, most of all, how *valuable* she could be to others. She could help save lives, he told her. Bring justice to those who'd long been denied. Ease their suffering. Let them find peace, and maybe a little happiness, at last.

Finally, then, she had a purpose in life, and in a place, the FBI, where she could grow.

Only, on this occasion, things didn't appear to be going very well for her. This first case she took part in beyond the walls of the J. Edgar Hoover Building was coming up empty. Nicks, the lead investigator, appeared to be a smart enough guy. But he was stymied, it seemed. There were no answers, either, that she could divine or comprehend for her part. Only a continued sense of frustration and sadness. And, as well, the distant voices that came to her when she least expected them, calling out to her whenever they wished, and lending to her their starry, cryptic signs.

Joanna... they whispered to her once more, even as she sat there brooding.

Go across the river.

She looked across the sprawling Connecticut, off to its far bank, where the town of Hadley began.

Go to Hadley this evening.

14

The New Search

It was 4:35 in the afternoon when John Henneger's cellphone rang. He fetched it from his belt holster, saw "Unknown" on the caller ID, then promptly ignored the incoming call.

Ten minutes later, the phone rang again. He checked it again. This time is was his boss. Since he was with a crew out in South Hadley working on a job and it was late afternoon, he figured the guy was calling to check on their progress for the day. Tapping on his phone's green answer button, Henneger put the phone to his ear.

"Yeah. John here."

His boss replied: "John. Where you at? You still on the job site?"

"Yeah. We'll be done in about an hour. What's up?"

"The FBI called, John. They're looking for you."

Shit.

"What the fuck for?"

"They didn't say. They said they called you on your cell, but you didn't answer."

Unknown.

"Fuckin' guys are harassin' me, Tom," Henneger snarled. "They keep gettin' after me."

"Yeah, well, you better get back to 'em. They said they need to get a hold of you."

What the hell was *that* all about?

Henneger rubbed his forehead. "I'll, uh, I'll call 'em back then."

"Okay. I'll see you when you get back here—or are you going straight home?"

Henneger considered his situation. "I'll be going straight home. Don't wait for me."

"K," said Tom. "See ya tomorrow."

The call ended.

Henneger eyed his phone for a moment, thinking things over. Then, deciding, he tapped it and navigated to his call history. His heart pumping and adrenalin filling his head, he tapped on the unknown number. The phone rang on the other end, and, after just two rings, the line picked up. A man with a southern accent answered.

"Special Agent Fielding."

Henneger took in a deep breath, then replied, "Returning your call. John Henneger."

"Ah, Mr. Henneger. Good to hear from ya."

I'll bet.

"Listen," Fielding went on, "we got us a search warrant for your house, here, in Northampton. We're here now, waitin' on ya. It'd be better for ya if you let us in."

"Searching for *what*?" Henneger asked.

"Ohh," Fielding said airily, "just some things—pictures and such. You could help us out a bunch and save us all a heap of time by coming by."

Henneger ran a few thoughts through his head. He couldn't think of anything in his house that'd tip 'em off to anything, but they could get lucky—or uncover something he hadn't thought of. And that warrant they had could be just the start of things.

"I got shit to do tonight," said Henneger. "Have fun at my place. You break anything, you own it—or you're payin' to get it fixed."

Fielding put on a surprised expression that Henneger couldn't see. "You sure about that, Mr. Henneger? You should probably be here."

"Why? To watch you guys tear up my place? I could use the insurance money. And you *will* be paying for anything missing or busted. I told you I was getting a lawyer."

After a couple more unpleasantries, Henneger hung up on the call. He put his phone in his holster, then looked all around him. He was in a parking lot at a minimart where he and his crew had been re-paving the front walkway. Across the street, over by an antique shop, he spied a state police cruiser parked on the street.

He was being watched.

Things were coming down to it, thought Henneger. Maybe the Feds were smarter than he'd guessed them to be, and them searching his house was his last warning to hit the road.

He looked back at his co-workers, still on the job of smoothing wet concrete off the walkway. "I gotta head out early, guys," he called out to them. "See you tomorrow."

They waved back and said their "see yas."

Henneger eyed the police cruiser again. He'd have to lose them guys somehow going back up north. Maybe make a stop in Hadley before bailing on them, he figured. He could always find another ride.

Walking over to his van that he'd parked off by the west side of the parking lot, he hopped inside. He started up the engine, then let it idle for a bit as he hatched his plan to get himself lost for a little while.

Maybe for a *very* long while.

****

Fielding walked back over to Nicks, who stood by the front door of Henneger's Northampton home along with two state police troopers. One of the officers carried a door-breaching battering ram. Also on the premises were three other state cops, a Northampton police officer, and one of the Boston field agents, Special Agent Seavers.

"He don't wanna be here," said Fielding to his partner. "Said he'll charge us for anything we break, though."

Nicks gave him an acknowledging nod, then turned to the trooper with the battering ram and pointed to the door. "Break it."

The trooper complied.

The door burst open on the first swing—sending pieces of wood and the door flange flying from the force of the strike.

Nicks, Fielding, and the two troopers entered the home. The two FBI agents kept their sidearms holstered, while both officers came in guns drawn.

"Clear the rooms," instructed Nicks just as the other state cops on-site came through the door. One of these troopers stayed posted by the door, while the others moved ahead to check out the rooms of the house.

Nicks looked around the room they'd first come into. It was a well-furnished living room with wall-to-wall carpeting, some cheap artwork on the walls, a couch, and a couple of cushioned chairs. Set at the opposite wall was a home entertainment center hosting a large, widescreen television. On the left side of the room, just before the entrance to the kitchen area, he noticed a wooden desk with a desktop computer on it. The desk fronted a window that looked out onto the backyard. A wooden chair was set before the desk.

Nicks pointed at the computer. "We'll take that with us," he said to Fielding.

Just then, Agent Seavers came into the house. Nicks turned to him. "Go check out the rooms over there," he said to him, pointing off to a hallway on the right side of the room that led to two bedrooms. The state cops were already busy in those, too, clearing them.

"Right," said the agent, heading off.

"I'll check out the kitchen," said Fielding.

"Good," said Nicks. "Grab any pictures or any other shit that might be stuck on his refrigerator."

Fielding gave him a nod.

With the search underway, Nicks strolled over to the window by the desk and looked outside. The backyard was wide, but the lawn itself was narrow, with a boggy forest behind it. This forest was part of a sprawling natural preserve that separated the residential neighborhood they were in from the banks of the Mill River, off to the south.

A state trooper strode by Nicks. "Checking the basement," he said as he went by him.

Nicks gave him a nod, then casually glanced around the room once more before his eyes settled on the desk in front of him. He stepped closer to it, then took a seat in the chair that was there.

The computer on the desk was an older model, probably six or more years old. A Windows machine. He picked up the keyboard and gave it a cursory peek underneath. Nothing. Then he looked at the desk's front end, and, seeing it had two small drawers, slid the both of them open. He rifled through each's contents. Both were packed with miscellaneous papers, old bills, spare pennies, and other assorted junk.

Fielding came out from the kitchen with his hands full. He tossed a small stack of photos on the desk in front of Nicks while clutching onto some other notes and photos he'd fetched from the refrigerator.

"Found those in a drawer in the kitchen," he said. "These," he said, hefting his clutch of paraphernalia, "were on the frigerator." He plopped them onto the desk, next to the stack of photos.

Nicks eyed the stack of photos. They were processed film photos, not the computer-printed variety. He took them up in his hands, and he examined one after another. He asked Fielding, "Anything else in there?"

"Just a couple of framed photos," said Fielding. "Stock shit. Looks like he bought most of his household goods from the Salvation Army."

"Yeah..." Nicks said as he perused the photos. "Check all the drawers in the house—bedrooms, basement, everywhere—for more of these," he said, waving the photos.

"Right."

The search went on.

This, Nicks knew, was the beginning of the last stage of their investigation. If they couldn't find anything to help pinpoint a new search area, then he'd be left with simply calling up the various local police departments and having them check a few places along the known routes going up to Loudon, New Hampshire. Other places closer by—maybe in the outlying towns—could also be searched. But none of the local cops, he figured, would be eager to run cold searches for the Feds. And that's all they had been doing, really, since they got there. Cold searches.

He pictured Sandy Whiting in his mind. The defiant woman deserved better than what she was getting from all of this.

They all did.

"More photos," said Fielding, coming up to Nicks. He plopped a shoebox onto the desk. "Found this in a walk-in closet in the bedroom."

Nicks put down the photos he was holding and picked up the shoebox. He set it on his lap, then began sifting through the stacks of photos inside.

"These look older..." he observed thoughtfully.

He glanced up at the computer. "Start taking this thing down," he said to Fielding. "Take it to the Northampton PD along with anything else we pack up."

Fielding went to work unplugging the computer and monitor and wrapping up their cords.

Nicks sat back in his seat and crossed a leg while cradling the shoebox in his lap. He picked through the photographs, some obviously quite old, others not so much. None of them appeared to have been printed from a computer, he noticed. A couple had dates on them: one read 1998, another 2001.

Sliding an older photograph from a sticky, faded batch, Nicks held it up for a better look. He saw that it was a photo of Lisa Saunders—though much younger looking than how she presented herself these days.

"Oh..." he mused, eyeing the photo curiously, "isn't this our Ms. Saunders, here?"

Fielding stopped what he was doing to check out the photo himself. "Yeah. Looks like."

Nicks shuffled through a few more photos in the sticky batch, peeling a couple of them apart from each other. "Here's some more," he said, examining them. He tossed one onto the desk as he took up the other one. Both photographs, he noted, had Saunders in them. In one of them, she was with a guy who didn't look familiar to him. He picked through a few more photos, then, most of which were nondescript and appeared to be of some camping trip or hike in the woods. Finally, then, he found two more that had a younger Saunders with a different group of people— one of whom, he noticed, was a more youthful version of John Henneger.

"Where'd you say you found these?" Nicks asked Fielding.

"The bedroom. There's a big walk-in closet in there. The box was on a shelf with some books."

Nicks kept picking through the photographs, his interest piqued.

Fielding hefted the computer monitor from the desk and carried it to the front door. Setting it down there, he then walked back to fetch the computer's tower to do the same.

Nicks, meanwhile, stopped at a photograph he'd just found. It was a shot of Lisa Saunders posing with an older couple. All three stood in front of a Christmas tree. The room they were in was quite dark—evidently to show off the Christmas tree's lights—but a hint of dim daylight shone through a window off to the left in the picture. Nicks eyed the scene curiously, then held the photo up and away from him. He slowly pivoted himself in his chair, still looking at the image.

Fielding, having brought the computer tower to the door, returned to the desk. "What's up?"

Nicks looked around the room, then at the photograph again, peering intently at some small detail in the image. Rising up from his seat, his gaze still locked on the photo, he began to slowly pace around the room, all the while holding the photo at arms-length in front of him.

Fielding watched his partner, puzzled by what he was up to.

Nicks glanced back and forth repeatedly from the photo to the room's walls. Then, stepping back towards the front door where the state trooper still stood by, he looked off to the far wall, at the home entertainment center. He looked at the photo once more.

"This photo of Saunders," he said, "was taken in here."

Fielding approached him. "Huh?"

Nicks stepped forward then, with Fielding following, to get a closer look at the far wall. He examined the wall's ceiling trim, then looked at the ceiling trim in the photograph, just noticeable by the Christmas tree's peak. It appeared to be the same style of trim. The window in the photo was also in just the right place.

"This photograph was taken in this house. In *this* room."

Fielding leaned in to examine the photo. "So then she lied to us," he said. "They must have hung out together outside of the bar."

Nicks' mind swirled. He looked down at the photograph again.

"This is old," he said, observing the photo's paper with its aging, yellowed back side. "This picture was taken fifteen, twenty years ago, I bet."

Fielding remained puzzled. "But Henneger didn't live here fifteen years ago."

Nicks pulled his gaze off the photo to look at Fielding, a sense of knowing overcoming him.

"Where did Saunders say she lived before moving into Henneger's house in Hadley?"

Fielding recalled, "Uh, downtown Northampton. In an apartment."

"Before that," Nicks replied.

"Before?" Fielding asked. Then his eyes flashed as it suddenly came to him, too. "Her aunt and uncle's house."

Nicks brought up the photo, showing it to his partner. "Meet Ms. Saunders' aunt and uncle."

"*Goddamn...*" Fielding swore.

Just then, Special Agent Seavers returned from going through the bedrooms.

"Nothing else back there," he said, coming up to Nicks.

Nicks showed him the photo of Saunders. "I want you to head out to see Ms. Saunders. Tell her we're inside Henneger's house, and we're searching it. Then ask her where her aunt and uncle lived—the address."

"Sure," said Seavers.

As he started off, Nicks turned to Fielding. "Call up the Guardian guys. We'll need their team out here. And we'll need to update our warrant, too, so get a hold of the judge."

Nicks looked off then to the state trooper by the front door. "Officer," he called out. The trooper looked at him. "Call your barracks. Tell 'em we need a cadaver dog out here."

The trooper gave a nod and got on his phone.

"You wanna pick up Henneger, too?" asked Fielding.

Nicks considering things. "No. Not yet. We've got him tailed. If he makes a run for it, we'll scoop him up. But right now I just want to be sure of things."

"All right."

Nicks ran things through his head. "Where's Agent Weirdlee at?" he asked.

"I dunno," replied Fielding. "I ain't heard from her all day."

"Call her up. Find out what she's up to."

"Sure thing."

While Fielding got on his cellphone, Nicks stepped over to the back window to look outside once more. The neighbors to either side, he recalled, were both several dozen yards distant, with their own properties consisting largely of heavily wooded areas. The forest preserve that lay beyond Henneger's back lawn, meanwhile, was thick and boggy, and would likely go undeveloped—and unexcavated—for generations.

The perfect place, Nicks surmised, for a secret burial ground.

15

Changing Plans

John Henneger drove up Route 47, his contingency plan
hatching in his mind. The ride was one of those where you
knew the route so well, you paid no mind to the scenery all
around you as it passed on by. The fields, the trees, the
manicured lawns, the small shops and little plazas that
decorated so many suburban neighborhoods. It was all
there. The everyday, peaceful life of America.

There was, however, no good place to hide anything out
there. No place for sure. Not and be absolutely certain that
no one else would ever come upon it. The only real way you
could know for sure is if you could be *right there*—or at
least somewhere nearby—and so be forewarned of it.

The walls were closing in on him, Henneger felt inside.
He'd taken a drunken risk the other night, cornering
Freddy like he did. Stupid. But the witch didn't do anything
beyond taking Freddy home, so he got away with another
one. Better, now, he figured, to disappear for a while, just in
case the Feds did get lucky, after all.

Slowly, his design came to him: First, he'd swing by
Angie's Dinner Inn, up on Route 9 in Hadley, where he'd
have himself a hearty meal and a couple of drinks. Then,
after eating—and with the staties hopefully remaining
outside waiting for him—he'd head to the restrooms and
slip out the back way, where from there a wooded area fell
away into a marshy wetland. Getting through that shit
might get messy, but afterwards he could make his way
through a few backyards and on down a couple of side
streets before arriving at his company's office and supply

yard. Trusted employee that he was, he had keys to all the trucks there. He'd just "borrow" one for his trip up north. By the time the cops figured everything out and Rocky discovered his truck missing that next morning, he'd be halfway into the northern hinterlands of Maine. After dumping the truck in some bog out there ("What? Somebody stole your truck, Rocky? That sucks."), his little disappearing act would be complete. Then, if the cops didn't find anything back in Massachusetts, he'd come back—albeit with some explaining to do regarding his van being left behind. Nothing a good ol' "none of your fuckin' business" couldn't take care of, though.

And if they *did* find something?

They'd never catch sight of John Henneger ever again. Not in this life, anyway.

Driving into Hadley, he looked into his rearview mirror as he turned onto Route 9, heading east. There, just one car behind him, was his state police escort. He grinned at the cruiser, thinking about all the stupidity on their part that had allowed him to get away with murder so for long, and how he was about to outsmart them again.

Some things never changed.

A mile up the road, Henneger pulled into the parking lot of Angie's. He found a space there next to a yellow Ford Focus. Getting out of his van, he eyed the little yellow car, which looked strangely familiar to him.

Ugly piece of shit, he said to himself.

The state police cruiser pulled into the parking lot after him. The trooper parked his vehicle off to the side.

Henneger strode purposefully into the restaurant.

Angie's Dinner Inn was a locally owned equivalent of an Applebee's. The place had a small, well polished bar area located at the right corner of the main dining room with enough room for a dozen guests to drink or have a meal there. The rest of the restaurant—which could host upwards of 100 people—was made up of rectangular dinner tables and a row of booth tables facing the establishment's large front windows. The whole place was dimly lit and had a colonial feel to it. Also, contrary to its name, Angie's didn't have any rooms available. The "Inn" part was just something the owner, Angie, wanted to include.

Henneger walked inside, his eyes roaming about the tables closest to him. The hostess by the doorway smiled and said "Hello" to him.

Initially, he'd wanted to eat at a table for more privacy, and was about to settle on one before he glanced to his right, across the room at the bar area. There, he did a double-take.

Was that the witch he saw there?

"Can I get you a table?" the hostess asked him.

He ignored her as he leered at the redheaded woman sitting at the bar, dressed finely in a dark skirt suit.

It *was* her, he determined.

"No thanks," he said to the hostess. "I'll just sit at the bar."

The hostess smiled at him as he stalked off.

Special Agent Weirdlee sat at the bar, dining at her leisure on a country chicken dinner. Henneger came up to her as she finished chatting with the woman bartender there. He noticed her dinner plate, along with what looked to be a chubby glass of bourbon or Scotch on the rocks for a drink.

"Well, well," he said to her, a wide grin on his face. "Look who we got here."

Weirdlee turned to him, appearing not the least bit surprised by his presence there.

"Mr. Henneger. Small world."

"Hell, yeah," he replied. He grabbed the bar chair next to Weirdlee's and turned it about to make room for himself. "Hope you don't mind if I sit here."

Weirdlee offered an accommodating nod and a wave of her hand. "It's a public place."

Henneger eyed her admiringly as he settled in and put his hands on the bar. She looked incredibly beautiful, with her skirt showing off more than enough leg, and that glistening maroon lipstick of hers perfectly complimenting her dark red hair.

She even *smelled* sexy.

"That was quite a little show you put on last night," he said to her.

"Show?" she asked, feigning bewilderment. "Whatever do you mean?"

Henneger chuckled. "You know—that trick you pulled in the alley? Fuckin' with my head."

"Mmmm," Weirdlee mused. "Trick, was it? I'm afraid I don't recall."

"Yeah," Henneger scoffed. "Right."

Weirdlee went back to eating her dinner, seemingly paying him no more mind.

Henneger, in turn, made no secret of his ogling eyes as he watched her.

"So..." he asked her then, "what brings you out here?"

She answered as she chewed. "Oh, just finishing up some work for the day."

He smirked at her. "Yeah. I bet."

The bartender came over. She wore a black golf shirt with the name "Angie's" embroidered on it.

"What can I getcha?" she asked Henneger.

He glanced at her—more like she was a bother to him than a server. "Budweiser and a menu."

"Sure," she said. She reached under the bar and grabbed a menu. She set in front of him, then went to fetch his beer.

Henneger brought his stare back to Weirdlee. He gave her a very slow, admiring once-over, savoring every inch of her slim, luscious body with his roaming eyes.

Damn, he told himself, *I've just gotta get me some of that shit.*

He smiled as his body warmed.

Maybe tonight, for sure.

****

"Ms. Saunders," called out Special Agent Seavers as he walked down the corridor at Cooley Dickinson Hospital.

Saunders, dressed in her nursing uniform, stopped and turned to him.

"Yes?"

Seavers produced his ID and showed it to her as he approached. "Special Agent Seavers, ma'am, Federal Bureau of Investigation."

Saunders immediately stiffened into a nervous pose as he came up to her.

"Can we talk for a moment, alone, please?" he asked her.

She glanced around, checking to see who might be watching them. "I guess so," she said. "I already said all I got to say, though."

"That's fine," said Seavers. "Just a couple more things."

That's what they always say!

Saunders nodded, then took him to the same break room where she'd talked to Weirdlee the other day. There, a couple of people were sitting at a table having coffee, so she led Seavers to a corner of the room where they could talk quietly.

"I'm just going to tell you what I told the lady," she said to him when they got there.

"Ms. Saunders," Seavers said, putting up a hand, "I'm here to tell you that we're searching Mr. Henneger's house—his Northampton home."

Saunders dead-stared at the agent.

"I was sent here to inform you of that, and to ask you if

there's anything you'd like to share with us before, maybe, we find something out for ourselves."

Saunders swallowed hard, and Seavers could plainly see the woman was under duress.

"I said all I got to say," she said once more.

"Ms. Saunders," Seavers asked her then, "where in Northampton did your aunt and uncle live? What street, I mean. You said you lived with them for a little while?"

Saunders muttered, "I, uh..."

"Your aunt and uncle, Ms. Saunders. What was their street address in Northampton? You lived there for a time, correct? While you were going to school?"

Saunders nodded uneasily. She answered, "I don't remember the number. It was a long time ago."

Seavers scoffed at that. "Your own relatives? Really, Ms. Saunders? You're telling me you can't remember what street you lived on for, what, two or more years?"

Saunders hesitated. In her mind, the whole horrible, ghoulish game she'd been playing for ten miserable years was finally nearing its end.

"Riverside," she muttered. "Riverside Drive."

"Was it 121 Riverside Drive, Ms. Saunders?" Seavers asked her.

She whispered back to him, "I don't remember the number."

Seavers checked the time on his wristwatch. It read 5:42 PM.

"You know," he said to Saunders, "it would go a lot better for you if you spoke to us now, if there's anything at all you think we should know."

Saunders shook her head vigorously. "No," she replied. Then she glanced about the room before saying to Seavers, "I think wanna talk to a lawyer."

"A lawyer?" Seavers asked. "So you think you need one?"

Saunders stepped away from the agent. "I gotta go," she

said to him. "I ain't got nothing else to say to you guys."

Seavers watched her as she hurried out of the break room. The woman, he guessed, was about to break. It was just a matter of time.

He reached for his smartphone to get back to Nicks.

****

Hadley Police Chief Towers arrived at John Henneger's house in Northampton, wanting to see for himself what Nicks was up to. He also reported to him that their search of the Fort River had come up empty.

Presently, the chief stood in the backyard along with Nicks and Fielding as all three watched the GPR team setting up their gear. The state police, meanwhile, had already put their cadaver dog to work sniffing about the left side of the property, heading into the woods.

"You really think he'd take a chance like this?" Towers asked Nicks. "Burying bodies in the backyard of somebody else's property?"

Nicks shrugged, looking off to the woods. "The owners weren't here at the time. They had a place down in Florida, so they were back and forth. And if that girl, Lisa Saunders, and Henneger were more than just bar friends, she could have helped him out."

Towers looked to either side of the property. "But the neighbors. That's a hell of a risk getting spotted."

Nicks shook his head, explaining, "Not any more so than anywhere else, really. Henneger had to get the bodies off of his property—and quick. I think that him calling up his pal, Saunders, and getting her involved, if he did, and then them possibly taking the women here was all just dumb luck on his part. Really just a panic move. Once they got the women here, though, Henneger might have thought to himself, 'fuck it—here is as good a place as any.' He knew that he had to hide them somewhere where no one would stumble across them by accident, and if they did start developing the land and digging things up, he'd be able to find out about it pretty quick. A place like this would be perfect for him. And Saunders' aunt and uncle selling the place in time for him to buy it? Icing on the cake. If the land back there ever did get searched or developed, he'd know about right away just by looking out his back window."

"Well, he knows about it now, doesn't he?"

"Yeah, he does. We told him we were searching his house."

"He could bolt on us."

"We've got that taken care of, Chief. Anyway, you remember earlier this week at the dump, when he drove up on us and raised all sorts of hell?"

"Yeah."

"Well, when he did that, I knew we were on the wrong track. He was comfortable enough to *go to us*, knowing we were digging up that landfill."

"So what?"

Nicks waved his hands around. "Now we told him we're searching his own house, and he's got no interest at all in being anywhere near us?"

Towers understood his meaning. "So we're getting close."

Nicks turned and pointed off to the woods. "I think we're at the bullseye, Chief, and those woods are it."

Just then, Nicks' smartphone rang. He pulled it out and answered it.

Seavers was on the other end.

After a couple of "yeahs" and "uh-huhs," Nicks said to him, "Follow her when she gets out of work, Special Agent. And make sure she knows it."

He tapped off his phone then and replaced it. Turning to Towers and Fielding, he said to Fielding, "Seavers just confirmed it. This was the woman's aunt and uncle's house." He looked at Towers. "She was living here when the Kerch women disappeared. That's for sure, now."

"Then that's it," Fielding said. "You want me to pick up Henneger?"

Nicks looked back at him. "No. I want to find those bodies first."

Towers shook his head uneasily as he gazed out at the darkening woods. "Ten years is a long time to be buried in the muck and dirt. Depending on how deep he put 'em, we'll be lucky if anything comes up."

Nicks started off back towards the house. "We got all night and then some to find out," he said. "This is the end of the road, Chief. Where else we gonna go tonight?"

Towers kept his eyes on the woods. "Yeah," he muttered, staring off into the eaves. "The end of the road."

****

Lisa Saunders got into her car and started for home. As she drove along, her eyes darted back and forth from her rearview mirror to the road ahead of her, again and again. The agent who had come to see her was following her now, she knew, and things were quickly getting out of hand.

Tears streamed down her cheeks. She mumbled to herself, "I didn't kill anyone. I swear I didn't kill anyone. I just want to go home..."

Around a corner she drove and almost through a red light—the agent following her sped on through it. She squeezed her steering wheel in her hands, then pounded it in frustration, screaming, "I want to go home! I didn't kill anyone!"

Yes, it was true, she hadn't killed a soul. But she *had* helped dispose of their bodies. And their cold, lifeless faces, contorted in their last expressions in life, were forever etched in her tormented mind. For ten long, agonizing years, they'd haunted her.

She would never be rid of them!

Saunders wept openly, begging them aloud, "Leave me alone," and imploring them to go away.

"I didn't kill you!"

It was the longest drive of her entire life. And the whole way, Special Agent Seavers stayed close behind her. Down a side street, back up another, until at last she arrived at her apartment building's parking lot.

Not waiting for Seavers to join her, she parked her car, grabbed her purse, then hopped out and ran up to her apartment door. Jostling her keys, she unlocked the door, hurried inside, and then locked the door behind her.

She had made it home. *At last.*

****

John Henneger found himself so perfectly at ease chatting with the witch lady, he ordered another beer for himself even after he'd finished his dinner.

Weirdlee was quite talkative on this night, philosophizing about the merits of learning a trade, as Henneger had done, and working towards becoming a homeowner. If only there wasn't the question of his involvement in the Kerch girls' disappearances, she mused.

Henneger assured her, though, that he was quite innocent in that regard.

"Sometimes, you know, chicks just get sick of your shit and they take off," he told her. "Happens all the time."

"Does it, really?" Weirdlee asked.

"Hell, yeah," he answered. His eyes ran down her lovely shape. "I bet you've kicked a few guys out the door in your day," he said with a smile.

Weirdlee took a sip from her drink. "I'm afraid I haven't had a whole lot of romance in my life," she said, and she eyed him suggestively before finishing, "so far."

Henneger let out a breath. "Shit. A hot chick like you? You gotta be lining 'em up."

"Not really," Weirdlee said. She leaned back in her chair and crossed her legs. "Not much of a charmer, I guess."

Henneger's eyes gravitated to her well-tanned, naked thighs. He swallowed hungrily, then carried his gaze to her slim waist and on up to her chest, where she'd left her white blouse unbuttoned just enough to allow for a generous view of her cleavage there. He imagined himself pressing close to her, feeling her soft, smooth skin against his own. "Some guys..." he said to her, seemingly entranced, "just don't know what to do with a beautiful woman."

She looked at him directly, offering a flattered smile. "You think so?"

Henneger licked his lips. "I never had that problem, myself."

She turned back to her drink. "I bet you don't."

Henneger kept his eyes on her. In his mind, he wanted to have sex with her so bad he could barely think of anything else. Not make love to her, mind you, but *fuck her*, good and hard. Rip off that blouse of hers, pull down that skirt—

"Do you play cards, Mr. Henneger?" Weirdlee asked him.

He snapped out of his daze. "Huh?"

She turned to him again. "Are you a card player at all?"

"Call me John," he offered, grinning wide.

"Okay, John. Why don't you call me Joanna, then."

He gave a nod. "Sure thing, Joanna."

"So? Do you play cards?"

"Yeah," he said. "You mean, like, poker?"

"Sure."

He smiled, showing off his yellowing teeth. "Strip poker, maybe."

She let out a laugh at that, saying to him, "Probably not." Then she glanced about the place, which by that time had a few more diners filling in the tables. "Not sure the company here would appreciate our entertainment."

Henneger had a solution to that problem. "We could always find someplace a little more, uh, private."

Weirdlee put up a finger, wagging it. "Tsk, tsk, John. Let's behave, now."

Henneger grumbled. He leaned over in his seat then, and he said to Weirdlee in a hushed voice, "Let me tell you something, lady. You are turnin' me on with that hot little body of yours. You ever hop in the sack with a wild man before?"

Weirdlee raised an eyebrow and drew herself back in her seat. "My, my. Aren't we forward."

"I'm serious," Henneger said. "You like bad boys, don't you? Don't tell me you don't."

Weirdlee looked him over, considering things, before turning to the bar and calling over the bartender.

The bartender walked up.

"Do you have a deck of cards?" Weirdlee asked her.

The bartender mulled, "Uhh, hang on. Lemme check."

As the bartender looked around, Weirdlee turned back to Henneger. "Let's stick with playing cards for now, shall we?" she said. "I tell you what. If I win, I get whatever money you have in your wallet."

"And if I win," Henneger said, "we get ourselves a room."

Weirdlee grinned back at him. Surprisingly, then, she offered an obliging nod.

"You know you want me to win," Henneger said to her confidently. "If they ain't got no cards here, I'll go out and buy a deck, myself."

They had cards. The bartender returned with an old used deck.

"High, low, jack, game?" Weirdlee asked as she shuffled the deck.

Henneger gave her a nod, "Sure," before adding, "No wild cards, though."

"Fair enough," said Weirdlee. "How about to eleven?"

Henneger smiled. "Sounds good." *The quicker we get this over with, the sooner I get to fuck your brains out.*

The two got to playing cards then and the young night wore on. Weirdlee ordered another of what she was drinking while Henneger pounded down beers. By 9:15 PM, the score was nine to seven, Henneger's lead. They'd both set each other multiple times, though, and Henneger was growing frustrated at not being able to close the deal. Eyeballing another crappy hand, he checked the time on his cellphone.

Fucking hell. He was pushing his luck.

He decided then to bid two, no matter what. Even if he got set again, he figured, that would still get him to eleven the surest way, excepting if Weirdlee caught up to him and actually won. And that latter scenario was a chance he was more than willing to take.

The reward—*that gorgeous witch*—was just too much to pass up.

16

Final Words

Truth be told, Special Agent Nicks wasn't always the confident, self-assured man he appeared to be while going about his duties at the Bureau. Same as anyone else, doubt occasionally clouded his mind, and at times—when the answers to a puzzle weren't so forthcoming and the truth lay especially vague—a simple educated guess was all he had to turn to.

More than confidence, then, it was about trust. Trust in the process. Trust in the knowledge you've acquired over time. Trust in the conclusions you came to based on determinations made from the only evidence you had to work with. Because sometimes, it was all you had to fall back on, and you just hoped it was enough to bring something to light.

The reason Nicks decided to become a cop in the first place, in fact, was due to his earlier teenage insecurities. Back in high school, he was never really much of a ladies man, and didn't get into sports at all, either. From early on, he much preferred the school's library to the break areas that most other kids hung out at. He was an avid reader—in particular of those "true crime" magazines and books. He loved the methodology of it all: Sifting through the evidence, weighing the forensics, judging the testimony of various witnesses—some trustworthy, others not so much. To him, it was all so logical, well ordered, and *comfortable*.

So when, after a couple of years of college, it came time for him to join the Pittsburg police force, he didn't do it for the same reasons that so many other macho cops joined the force—to wear a badge, carry a gun, and boss people around. He wasn't the least bit interested in any of that part of law enforcement. Instead, for him, it was all about crime scene investigating. That's it. And it wasn't so very long before he became quite good at it, on his own.

The FBI came later. Normally, it's not easy getting into the Federal Bureau of Investigation. But Nicks had a solid reputation to back him up along with a string of cleared homicide investigations and other cases to burnish his résumé. As a result, he quickly found a place for himself in that organization, too.

Most people are of the mind that because homicide detectives go through so many cases, they must eventually become numbed by the brutality they bear witness to in the course of their jobs. In reality, though, that just isn't so. Eventually, over time, just like any combat veteran, the horror of it all becomes embedded in your soul. It becomes part of an everyday struggle to survive, psychologically, in a world where sometimes the bad people win the day.

And, as well, you come to absolutely despise those who have wrought such evil upon the innocents you've seen slain. You want justice for the victims—and much more so than when you were a kid in high school reading all those cheap true crime magazines and treating everything so clinically, as if it were all just a puzzle to be solved and nothing more.

For Nicks, these days, it *was* more.

And it was terrible, all the time.

"Nicks."

Special Agent Fielding tapped his partner's shoulder.

Nicks had gone back into Henneger's house soon after the search and recovery teams had arrived on site. Putting his feet up on the desk inside the living room to rest a while, he'd soon thereafter nodded off into a half-dream. He snapped awake, now, his head darting about as he caught his bearings.

He looked up at Fielding, standing over him. "Yeah?"

Fielding wore a drawn expression on his face, as if his own youthful innocence had just been stolen away from him. He whispered to Nicks in a solemn, heartbroken voice.

"Found 'em."

Nicks got up quickly from his chair. The darkened interior of the house, he saw, was lit up with the flashing reflections of blue and white police lights coming from outside, where a half dozen police cruisers, both state and local, crowded the street and Henneger's driveway. An ambulance was also parked on the street.

Nicks followed Fielding as the two men made their way into the kitchen and out the back door. The backyard was lit up by police spotlights, most of them aimed at the shadowy woods beyond the yard. The two agents stalked purposefully across the yard and into the woods. Police officers stood at intervals, and a few plainclothes cops walked to and fro as Nicks and Fielding proceeded.

A hundred yards into the trees then, the agents came upon a crowd of police officers all huddled around a gaping hole in the ground. The Guardian GPR team was off to the side, packing up their gear. The cadaver dog sat beside his keeper over by a tree. There, also, was parked a mini backhoe that had dug the hole into the bog, unburying its darkest secret.

Hadley Police Chief Towers was there, too, his watery eyes locked on the freshly dug hole. He held his hat over his heart, and he crossed himself as he muttered weakly, "Jesus, Mary, Joseph, God help them..."

Nicks looked down into the hole. A forensics team was

there, examining the decrepit remains of a heavily wrapped bundle.

"Two women," Fielding said to him. "One mature, the other younger."

For what seemed an eternity, Nicks stared down at the terrible scene below him, alone with his own heartache as the cold reality of the week's investigation slowly sank into him.

It was over, finally.

****

"Son of a bitch," Henneger swore.

Weirdlee smiled as she tallied up the final score—eleven to seven, her win.

"Don't worry, John," she said to him, "you can keep your money."

"Fuck," Henneger swore again, slapping the bar's top in frustration. "I thought for sure I was gonna beat you, girl."

"Oh, well," Weirdlee said. "Win some, lose some."

She gathered up the cards into a stack and set the deck on the bar.

Henneger eyed her then with a mischievous grin. "Well, shit," he said, regaining his lust for her, "we could still shack up, you know. How about I buy you a shot?"

"Oh, I'm sorry," Weirdlee said to him, "but I never drink on duty." And with that, she took her half-filled chubby glass and downed its contents in one long, single gulp. It was easy for her to do, actually, since she hadn't been drinking bourbon or Scotch or whatever else Henneger imagined her drinking, after all. Instead, it was merely her favorite soda, Dr. Pepper. A quick arrangement with the bartender prior to Henneger's arrival had set everything up.

Henneger stared at her, bewildered in his own drunken

state. "What do you mean you're on duty?"

"I don't have office hours, John," she explained. "I just work until they don't need me anymore."

Henneger eyed her coolly. "So..." he asked, "when you gettin' off duty?"

Weirdlee looked off behind Henneger, there to see Hadley Police Sergeant Banning and another local officer coming in through the door.

"Right about now, actually."

Henneger smiled at first—until he noticed Weirdlee's gaze looking past him. He spun about in his chair, there to see Banning and the other cop walking up to him.

"What the fuck?" he swore at the officers.

Banning scowled at him. "Henneger," he said to him in a seething tone, "Get up off that chair."

"Fuck you," Henneger answered.

Banning grabbed hold of him and forced him up while the other officer kept a hand on his holstered sidearm.

"This is bullshit!" Henneger swore at Banning as the officer spun him about and brutishly handcuffed him.

Banning said back to him, "You're under arrest for the murders of Suzanne and Rebecca Kerch, you piece of shit. We got your ass."

Weirdlee got up from her chair. She looked at Henneger, her smile having left her. "Good night, Mr. Henneger."

Henneger glared back at her, his face contorted in rage. He growled, "You miserable bitch."

She leered back at him contemptuously, and she flashed her eyes and replied to him, quite satisfied, "*Witch*, you say!"

Then, as Banning and the other officer manhandled their captive towards the door, Henneger shouted out for all in the place to hear:

"That fuckin' girl's a witch! She's a witch! Look at her!

She's a fuckin' witch! She's a *WIIIITCH!*"

The patrons stared at Henneger as the cops pulled him out the door. They looked off, then, towards the bar where he'd been sitting before.

No one was there.

****

It was 10:45 PM when Sandy Whiting's cellphone rang in the darkened motel room. Jarred awake by its ringing, Richard grabbed the phone from the nightstand and answered it.

"Yes?" he asked.

He listened as Special Agent Nicks spoke to him on the other end. He replied in a choked voice, "All right."

He rolled over then and nudged his wife, sleeping next to him in bed. Sandy awakened, groggy, and turned to her husband. He didn't have to say a word to her as he handed her the phone. The expression on his face said it all.

The phone call Sandy Whiting had been waiting ten long years for had finally arrived.

Her wails of anguish filled the evening air.

****

Special Agent Seavers stood by with a Massachusetts State Police trooper outside the apartment of Lisa Saunders.

Seavers pounded on the door.

"Ms. Saunders," he called out. "Open the door, ma'am."

The trooper peeked inside the window, but none of the lights were on so he couldn't make out anything.

Seavers banged on the door again. "Ms. Saunders, open the door."

Nothing.

Just then, a Florence police cruiser, its headlights flashing in the darkness, came speeding into the parking lot and came to a screeching halt before the front walk of Saunders' apartment. From the passenger side leapt a plainclothes officer, waving a paper in his hand. "Got it," he shouted. A uniformed female officer jumped out of the driver's side, and the both of them ran up the steps.

Seavers pounded on the door once more. "Ms. Saunders! We have a warrant for your arrest. Open the door."

Still no response.

The plainclothes Florence cop came up to stand next to Seavers. The uniformed officer drew her pistol and positioned herself at the foot of the steps, on guard. Then Seavers, the plainclothes officer, and the state trooper all drew out their own sidearms.

Seavers looked at the state trooper. "Bust it open."

The trooper obliged.

After two hard kicks, the door burst open, and the officers all rushed inside.

Seavers found the light switch by the door and slapped it on. The state trooper and plainclothes cop hurried across the living room first and then entered the small kitchen area. The uniformed Florence officer remained by the front door.

"Clear," said the trooper in the kitchen area. Then he, the plainclothes cop, and Seavers converged upon the right-side hallway that led to the apartment's bathroom and single bedroom. After quickly checking the opened bathroom, Seavers and the trooper stood off to either side of the closed bedroom door.

"Ms. Saunders?" Seavers called out.

Again, silence.

Seavers gave the trooper a nod, and the officer drew up

and kicked open that door, too.

All three men hurried inside.

Saunders, dressed in a nightgown, lay in her bed. Beside her, on her cluttered nightstand, lay her opened purse. Beside that was an emptied pill bottle and an empty glass.

"Call an ambulance!" Seavers yelled as he ran over to her side. He quickly checked her pulse. Nothing. He picked up the pill bottle then and read that it was for sleeping pills. He grabbed the empty glass and sniffed it. It smelled of vodka.

While the plainclothes cop busied himself calling for an ambulance, the state trooper started CPR on Saunders. An effort, however, that would be in vain.

Lisa Saunders was dead.

Seavers glanced about the nightstand. There, he noticed a small piece of paper set beside the empty vodka glass. Seeing something written on it, he leaned over to read it what it said.

The paper read:

> *John Henneger killed Suzy and*
> *Becky Kerch.*
> *I helped him bury their bodies.*
>
> *I AM GOING TO HELL*

17

Going Home

With the discovery of the bodies of Suzanne and Rebecca Kerch, prosecutors were able to charge John Henneger with two counts of homicide. Their case would be strengthened by the suicide note left by Lisa Saunders, as well as the statement provided by Fred Duncan which effectively eliminated Henneger's only alibi. Other witnesses—guilt-ridden in their own right for having kept quiet for a murderer—would also come forward to corroborate Duncan's recollection of time and events. Why Saunders had chosen to become involved in Henneger's grisly double murder by helping him cover it up remained a mystery. Nicks speculated that she may have been a buyer back in Henneger's drug dealing days, and may have owed the man a debt.

The truth, however, would never be known.

As for Henneger, he tried at first to deny everything—blaming it all on the deceased Saunders. Forensics results from the murder victims' remains, however, indicated that it would have taken a person of considerable strength to inflict the fatal injuries discovered on them. There was no evidence, furthermore, to suggest any other possible suspect or accomplice present in either Henneger's Hadley home or his Northampton property.

And so by the spring of that following year, John Henneger would be convicted of the murders of Suzanne and Rebecca Kerch, and would spend the rest of his natural born life in prison.

****

On the Friday morning following the previous night's arrest of Henneger, Special Agents Nicks, Fielding, and Weirdlee stood outside the Northampton Police Department headquarters, chatting it up just prior to their departure. While the two men wore their usual dark suits and ties, on this morning—in contrast to days prior—Weirdlee notably wore a white pantsuit.

"I'll be glad to get home for the weekend," said Fielding. He glanced at Weirdlee, then to Nicks. "Miss my wife, you know."

Nicks gave him a nod. "Yeah."

A car drove up quickly then and parked alongside the curb. Out of the vehicle leapt Sandy and Richard Whiting.

Sandy yelled out as she ran up to the FBI agents. "I would have kicked myself in the ass if I missed you guys!"

They all smiled at that.

Sandy came first to Nicks, and she threw her arms around him, hugging him tightly for a few precious moments. The others looked on, understanding. Pulling herself away then, tears streamed down her cheeks as she looked into his eyes. "My hero," she whispered to him. "Thank you *so* much."

Nicks replied to her sincerely, "I'm really glad we could help you."

Sandy went over to Fielding next, and she hugged and thanked him. Then she hugged and thanked Weirdlee, in turn. Richard followed behind her, and shook each agent's hand.

"Thank you all," Sandy said to them, and she finished in a choked voice, "I can't believe this has finally happened." She eyed them all for a moment, wiping tears from her face as she recovered herself. "We'll be taking Suzy and Becky back to Connecticut," she said. "They'll be with us, now."

Nicks said back to her, "They were always with you, Mrs. Whiting."

She nodded. "Yeah." Then she clutched onto her husband's arm. "Will we be seeing you again?" she asked Nicks.

He replied, "Probably at the hearings, ma'am. Me, anyway."

"Okay, then," she said with a smile. Then she waved at all the agents. "Thank you all again. You're all our heroes. We'll never forget you."

She and Richard went back to their car then and hopped inside, and Richard fired it up. He pulled away from the curb, and off they drove, to get on with their lives.

Fielding said to Nicks, "Well, that about wraps things up, partner."

Nicks gave a quick nod. "Looks like." Then he turned to Weirdlee and said to her, "Thanks for all your help on this one, Joanna. It was nice having you around."

"*Joanna?*" Weirdlee smiled. "Wow—a first name basis, at last."

Nicks laughed. "Sure. Why not?"

Fielding put his hands in his pockets. He said to Weirdlee, "Good luck to ya, Agent Weirdlee. Maybe we'll work together again sometime."

"Oh," Weirdlee replied, "I'm pretty sure we haven't seen the last of each other, *Agent* Fielding."

He looked at her curiously. "Ya think so? That yer woman's intuition telling ya that?"

She smiled coyly. "Something like that."

"So," said Nicks to her, "you heading straight back to D.C. from here?"

She shook her head. "No. I'm taking the turnpike east, actually, to visit with my mom and dad—if they'll see me, anyway."

"Oh?" Nicks said. "Problems with the folks?"

She nodded. "Long time, now."

"Sorry to hear that."

"It's okay," she said. "We'll work it out someday, I guess."

Weirdlee glanced behind her, towards the direction of Main Street. "Well, I've got something else to take care of before I go." She looked at Nicks and Fielding. "Nice working with you gentlemen."

"Same here," said Nicks.

The agents shook hands and said their farewells then, and Weirdlee stepped away.

Nicks and Fielding both watched her as she made her way toward Main Street.

"That is one interesting woman," quipped Fielding. "Mysterious, ya know?"

Nicks grinned at him. "Yeah, and not too shabby looking, either."

Fielding faked a scowl. "I told you, Agent Nicks, I'm a happily married man."

Nicks laughed. "So you are, Danny boy. So you are."

****

O'Brien's Pub opened its doors at 11:00 AM each morning, and you could count on the same collection of regulars wandering in before noontime arrived. Freddy Duncan, naturally, was one of them. All he had to do was walk into the place, and the bartender already had a beer popped open and set in front of him by the time he sat down at the bar.

"Morning, Fred," said the bartender on this morning, a skinny woman in her early forties, with faded tattoos decorating her arms.

He smiled back at her, happy to be there. "Hi, Sally."

He grabbed hold of his ice-cold brew as he settled into

his usual seat. *Mmmmm.* What else could a guy ask for on a perfect Friday afternoon?

The doorway jingled every time another patron came in, and Freddy didn't pay the jingling any mind as he nursed his first beer of the day.

"Good morning, Fred," said Agent Weirdlee to him.

He stopped at mid-slurp, quickly turning to see his darling FBI girl standing there, dressed beautifully in her white outfit.

"Hi!" he said to her, beaming.

She smiled at him, and stepped closer to his side. "I'm leaving today, so I just wanted to say goodbye, and say thank you for helping us out."

He chuckled. "Thanks for what? I didn't do nothin' special."

"You sure did, Fred," she insisted.

He shrugged and turned himself back to his beer. "It wasn't so much, what I did. I only wanted to..." He stopped himself, not wanting to get mushy on her. "I'm glad you got Johnny in jail. He's a bad guy."

Weirdlee nodded. "He's very bad guy, Fred. And what you did for us was a very brave thing to do, you know."

"Naw..." Fred said. "I was scared to death the whole time."

Weirdlee put her hand on Fred's shoulder. "That's what makes it brave, Fred. When you do something you know is right, even though you're scared."

Fred took a swig from his beer and shook his head. He didn't believe her.

"Hey, Freddy!" called out a guy from across the bar. "Drink up, my man!"

Fred gave him a nod and a fractured smile, and then glanced sheepishly at Weirdlee. After all his years spent hunched over a bottle, he had no spirit left in him, and when he looked at her, he saw a woman who was *way* out of his league, just as he had heard before.

"I'm not a brave guy at all," he said to her in a meek voice. "I'm just a...a dumb drunk in a bar."

Weirdlee's smile faded. She gazed, quite solemnly, at the broken man before her.

"I think you're a *very* brave man, Fred Duncan," she said to him. And she pressed herself close to him. "I think you're a very *good* man, too."

Then she leaned in closer, still, and she whispered sweetly into his ear, *"You always have been..."*

And she kissed him gently upon his cheek.

Fred's mouth went agape—and for a moment he felt entirely unable to speak! For all at once, his entire body convulsed, and the muffled world around him came alive with vibrant sounds, while his vision, once blurry, instantly cleared!

"*WHAAT...?*" he gasped—it was all he could think of to say!

Weirdlee smiled and winked at him. "Bye, bye, Freddy." And she stepped away towards the door.

Fred spun about in his chair, and he called out to her, "Joanna!"—As if he had always remembered her name!

She turned to him with a genuine smile.

He cried out to her, "Thank you!"

"Good luck to you, Fred Duncan," she said back to him. "Have a good life."

And with that, she twirled herself around and sauntered carefree through the door.

So it was that Special Agent Joanna Weirdlee—aka Joanna Osborne, she descended of witches and sorceresses from times untold and ancient—left O'Brien's Pub, never to be seen there again.

Fred turned himself back around, still taken aback by

what had just occurred. He looked down at his beer, and then he stood up from his seat. He fetched his wallet from his back pocket and pulled out some money.

"You want another?" asked Sally.

"No," he replied to her. "I'm all set, thanks."

He glanced around at the others there—all the people who had no place better to be—before looking back at the bartender. "I'm going to see my daughter tomorrow."

She smiled at him. "Yeah. See you in the afternoon."

No, he said to himself, picturing his dear, sweet Kelly in his mind.

Not this time.

He placed his money on the bar, and he slid his beer away. Then he looked all around, once more.

"See ya later, guys," he said to everyone there.

Then he strode to the door and swung it open with glee. He stepped outside and glanced around—smiling to himself, as he knew better than to think the witch from Salem might still be there. And so he pranced down the sidewalk with a spring in his step, and he ran up to people he knew, merrily greeting them as they looked back at him with bewildered faces.

Freddy Duncan was healed, and the joy and happiness he felt inside of him would be with him, always, for the rest of his very long, and very happy, life.

- - -

If you enjoyed *Cold Case: FBI – The Salem Witch*, please consider reviewing it online.
Reviews play an important role in the placement of books at online retailers.

****

Book 2 in the series...

Cold Case: FBI - The Curse of the Bayous

Deep in the Louisiana bayous, a poor single mother has lost her little boy, gone missing during a community outing attended by the boy's father, her estranged husband. Three years later, FBI special agents Sam Nicks, Danny Fielding, and Joanna Weirdlee arrive to investigate the missing boy's case gone cold. Agent Weirdlee, however, soon finds herself at odds with a powerful and murderous voodoo priest, whose own desire to subdue the Salem witch threatens to destroy her life before she's even begun to realize her true supernatural powers.

www.ingramcontent.com/pod-product-compliance
Lightning Source LLC
Chambersburg PA
CBHW060209180626
46813CB00007B/2760